WEDDING FEVER

PATRICE WILTON

DEDICATION

I would like to thank Community Authors, and in particular my editor, Traci Hall for brainstorming with me and doing a wonderful editing job, and Christopher Hawke for his work creating my manuscript into print book format.

On a personal note, I'd also like to thank my partner, Ralph, for his patience when I'm working long hours each day and constantly obsessing over my book, and lastly, love to all my family, and hugs and kisses to my darling grandchildren.

PROLOGUE

I'm Cupid, the little guy with the bow and arrow and an aim that has yet to miss. I reside in the idyllic town of Serendipity Falls where I go about my love-making business without any trumpets or flair. Strangely enough, considering the huge impact I have on people's lives, my existence remains unknown. At times this bothers me, but mostly I ignore the whisperings about the so called "love bug" believed to be in the spring water. I used to stamp my feet and get livid over this insult to me and my skills, though with my one hundred percent success rate, I've learned to smile with indulgence. For after all, I know that I am the one who brings them joy and happiness, and what could be a greater gift, or a better legacy than that? Yes, I am truly blessed.

In Cupid years, I'm a mere 180 years old, for we tend to live to be 500 or greater, especially if we take care of ourselves and don't over indulge in daily human pleasures. Take chocolate for example. It's one of my favorite treats, as is a nip of brandy in my hot cocoa each night. I also love nibbles of fine cheese, buttery croissants, home baked cookies, and admit a certain weakness to M&Ms.

But I digress. I'm here to tell you about the most magical place on earth, our very special Serendipity Falls in the foothills of Mammoth, California. The town gets its name from the beautiful falls that cascade down the side of the mountain, pooling into an emerald green lake. There's an excellent restaurant with a perfect view of the falls, and in the center of town we have a super new mall with plenty of activity. I float between both places looking for lonely strangers to unite.

Oh, wait. I see a prospect now. The lovely girl is the one who runs the boutique aptly named Wedding Fever. She pretends to believe in love and happy endings, but I know differently. There's a piece of her heart that is broken and she guards it carefully. Perhaps today I can help mend it. Nothing would give me greater pleasure than watching the miracle of love blossom inside that sassy young gal. Now—who to be her mate?

CHAPTER ONE

Mila O'Reilley had her key in hand, ready to open her shop and welcome more ridiculously happy and eager brides-to-be, when a young man scooted forward and shoved a mic in her face.

"Excuse me, Miss, but I'm Chase Carlton with the San Francisco News. May I ask you a few questions?"

She sighed, then turned slowly to face yet another reporter. How many had it been? At least half a dozen in the past couple of months. "What's with you guys? Don't you have anything more important to report?"

"No, I'm afraid not." The man gave her a confident smile. "This is the biggest story to hit these parts since the Gold Rush."

She laughed in surprise, accepting the truth in his statement. People *were* showing up in Serendipity Falls seeking their happiness just as they had come searching for gold more than a century and a half ago. "That's pretty pathetic, isn't it?"

"Not sure. Depends if they find what they're looking for."

At his deeper tone, she raised her eyes from the key in her hand. His innocent blue gaze twinkled merrily. He looked so young…so indecently naïve and unprotected. Her underdog instincts kicked to the forefront as she imagined him fresh meat for the eager-beaver ladies on the prowl, hoping to find a husband.

A wave of sympathy moved her for this man's plight. She'd seen stronger men than him succumb to the mysterious force of nature that drove them to their knees.

"I suppose you're right." She licked her dry lips. A cute guy like him would be a babe magnet for sure. Married or not. Willing or not. "But what if they aren't looking? If this is the last thing they want?"

"They can always leave," he chuckled. "Nothing is forcing them to stay."

"I'm not sure about that. Sometimes I think the men and women in this town have lost their will to decide for themselves. Not that someone is holding a gun to their heads or anything but…I grew up around here and never in my life did I see so many people itching to get married. Even my own brother."

"Lost their will--that's an interesting thought. Care to expound?"

She shook her head. "No. I probably said too much already." She looked at the lone cameraman. "Cut that, will you?"

He jerked his chin to Chase, who nodded. "If you insist, but I would love to delve deeper into this. Your own brother was a victim?"

She winced. "I'm late opening, so if you're done with your questions…"

"Just a few more if you can spare the time?" He gave her a dimpled smile, one she was sure had bought him plenty of favors in the past. But he was in dangerous territory now—a predatory environment, and if he continued to flash that smile around here, he'd be toast, or at least a trophy on some young woman's arm.

Immune to his charms, she cocked her head and pursed her lips, studying him for a moment. Should she warn him or let him learn the hard way? Serendipity Falls was her town, and she felt an obligation to protect him from getting caught in some cougar's net. "What would you like to know?"

"Your name for starters."

"Mila O'Reilley," she answered, wishing all the questions would remain this easy.

"Ms. O'Reilley, thank you for your time." He spoke smoothly, in an easy, confident news reporter voice. "The people flocking to Serendipity Falls have no inhibitions as to why they've come. They want to fall in love and have the kind of marriage that doesn't end in divorce. Why here? What makes this place special?"

"No idea. Your guess is as good as mine."

He beamed a smile so bright that she had to blink.

"You work at this bridal boutique and come in contact with happy young couples every day. I'd call that insider's knowledge. They must talk to you, perhaps share details of how they met and fell in love."

Mila was not about to discuss her customers and the sweet, if slightly torrid stories they told her. She was the proprietor of the boutique she'd named "Wedding Fever" and it was doing a lively business. She didn't intend to kick a gift horse in the mouth. "It's different for everybody," she replied. "As it is everywhere."

"Well, in your *expert* opinion, would you say that there's a love bug in the spring water?" He stepped between her and the door, effectively shutting off her means of escape.

"No. Of course not." She didn't like being put on the spot, or forced to do something she had no wish to do. Like discuss the mania surrounding Serendipity Falls. This interview was over. "That sounds silly, doesn't it?" She ducked under his arm and had the key in the door.

"You must have some theory," he said sharply, obviously not willing to give up. "If not a bug, what is it? Viagra in the Falls?"

She turned her head and grinned. "That's clever. I like that. You should use it in your report."

A dimple flashed. "Give me something to work with here. What are your ideas?" His eyes trailed down her face, past her neck, over her fleece jacket and back up again. They lingered on her mouth. "Don't be shy. Our readers want to know what's causing this mad dash to the altar—especially all the young single women."

He leaned in closer and Mila felt herself trapped once again. "Single women require single men. Most of the time."

"Come on," he coaxed, gifting her with his dimple once more. "You must admit it's odd. The amount of weddings that take place here–you have to know something."

She sighed, resigned to the fact she had to play nice in front of the camera. "Lately, it seems like an epidemic," she said glancing nervously at the cameraman, "but in a good way."

"You mentioned your brother. Had he known his bride long?"

Devon and Tara would be furious to hear her talking about them on the nightly news, but she had thoughtlessly mentioned them and now had to answer. "They're getting married in two weeks, but he proposed after about a month which is almost a lifetime around here."

He laughed. "Really? So things do move along quickly."

Mila nodded. "They sure do. My brother actually took it slow considering that he fell in love the first time they met. She's wonderful."

"True love?" Chase's brows lifted in disbelief. "In such a short time?"

"Yes. Sometimes you just know." As the cameraman zoomed in on the sign above her shop, she realized how good this unexpected exposure might be for her business and decided to play it for all it was worth. "It's just so romantic around here," she sighed dramatically and pretended to wipe a tear from her eye. "It truly is a miracle." She gave him a teasing smile. "You're cute — you might need to be careful. Are you married?"

"No." He laughed–an unbeliever. "I'm not worried. The last thing I want is to get hitched. Are you?"

"No, not me." Single and happy. Period.

"You're young and attractive…"

"No time to date," she answered quickly, eager to turn the conversation away from herself. "I have too many weddings to plan," she added.

"Is it at all possible that this is a myth created by the locals to bring tourists to Serendipity Falls?" he asked.

Her head shot up and heat rose in her cheeks. "No!"

He gave an apologetic smile. "I'm sorry to ask, but I'm trying to uncover the truth. The town suffered once the mines were closed. It turned into a pit stop on the way to the ski hills."

Mila gathered her composure, aware of the camera. He wasn't nearly as naïve as she'd first thought. It would serve him right if the love bug bit him hard and trapped him for good.

"What are you implying?" Her eyes narrowed slightly. She might agree with him in private, but no way in hell would she sit by and let some out-of-towner poke fun, or question the integrity of the people she worked and lived with. This was her home, damn it. And whatever *it* was, it certainly was bringing a lot of happiness to Serendipity Falls. Not to mention a boost to the economy.

"I'm asking, in your opinion, if the love bug is real? Or is this some kind of elaborate hoax?"

If the camera wasn't rolling, she'd tell him what she really thought. Hanging on to her temper by a thread, she shook her head. "No tricks here. This is the real deal."

"What do you mean by that?"

She looked directly at the camera and spoke, "We have at least a couple of weddings a month in a town of 10,000, and no divorces as far as I know. Where else can you say that?"

His smile turned smug. "You'd know those stats best. After all, you are the manager of this boutique, the Wedding Fever. Correct?"

Mila bristled. "Owner, not manager, and the numbers I gave you are simple facts." She tossed her head. "Could actually be higher since we have so many. If you don't believe me go see for yourself. The weddings are on record at the city hall." She turned the key in the lock and leaned against the door jamb, ready to slip inside and slam the door behind her the second he gave her an inch.

"Why wouldn't I believe you? Even if you're profiting from this crazed rush to the altar, there is no denying that it's happening. The question is why?" He glanced down at her right hand. "Tell me something. How did a pretty woman like you escape?"

Another comment on her looks. Sheesh! As if that was a recipe for love. This charming reporter boy was an idiot and she'd wasted enough time answering his silly questions. Heavy on the sarcasm she answered, "Just lucky, I suppose."

He gave her a wolfish smile. "You suggested I should be careful. Think I'm in danger?"

She smiled, saccharin sweet. "I changed my mind. Someone as skeptical as you would scare away anyone remotely interested in romance."

"Whoa. You know how to hurt a guy." His smile slipped from his overly handsome, clean cut face. He looked like a city boy through and through with his blond hair spiked and none of the facial growth that real mountain men favored. His lips were full and sensual, his jaw strong, and he had long girly lashes framing clear, sky blue eyes. Attractive, yes, but she preferred dark haired men- the rugged outdoor types.

"My apologies. Not everyone around here is driven by their lust or emotions." She certainly wasn't, but to run her business successfully she had to pretend otherwise. She could gush and coo as enthusiastically as anyone when love birds waltzed in, and happily oblige in making all their dreams come true.

"I'm not a cynic," he told her, as if sharing a secret between just them, and a hundred thousand viewers. "I believe in love as much as the next person." He gave a careless shrug. "I'm just here to do a report and find out the truth behind this legendary town. People are moving in by the droves and real estate has spiked."

"That's true," she conceded. "Things are looking up." She turned her back to him and quickly cracked open the door. "Why don't you drop by the store later and meet some of the happy couples yourself. Get their take on things."

"I'll do that. Thanks for your time--it was a pleasure speaking with you."

He glanced at his cameraman. "That's a wrap. Let's grab a few interviews from these people strolling by." He took a step then stumbled backwards.

"Ouch!" He grabbed his chest, looking like he was about to keel over. "What was that?"

"What?" she asked, more curious than worried.

"A sharp pain right over my heart." He straightened up, obviously trying to compose himself. "I'm sure it's nothing."

"If your chest hurts perhaps you should call a doctor."

He patted his chest, but was breathing fine. "It's still smarting."

"Might be the love bug," she suggested with an innocent smile.

"I'd prefer a heart attack," he answered back.

"A heart condition at your age? Well, it does happen." Playing the devil's advocate, she added, "On a happy note your photographer could give it a different slant. "Love bug kills reporter at mall." Could make you famous. Not rich though."

"I'm in perfect health. Or was until a minute ago. You don't think *it's that*, do you?" he asked anxiously, rubbing at his chest. "I didn't drink the bottled spring water, but if it's airborne this thing could be inside the mall." He glanced upward, like he was expecting to see something floating overhead. "No. That's ridiculous. Couldn't happen." He glanced at the cameraman. "Don't film this. Okay?"

Mila couldn't resist teasing him some more. "Since it's never happened to me, I wouldn't know. I make sure I wear protective armor under my clothes."

"You do? Mind if I report that?"

"No, of course you can't. I'm kidding." She whispered, "Besides, I only have on a bra. Pink," she told him, and was pleased when he blushed. "What is your name again? And which news station do you work for?"

"Chase Carlton with the San Francisco WUX News." He ran a hand through his spiked hair. "Pain's receding now. I must have had a muscle spasm."

"Well, Chase Carlton with WUX News. Drop in later. Hopefully you'll get to meet one of our lucky ccuples."

When he didn't reply, she glanced at him closely. "You okay? Your face is flushed and you have a feverish look in your eye."

"I'm fine. Feel quite good, actually." He blinked, and blinked again. He took a step forward nearly bumping into her. "Did anyone ever tell you that you are extremely beautiful? Your eyes sparkle like diamonds, and your lips are pink and lush."

"Oh, no!" She rolled her eyes. "You got it. Get away from me. You've been bitten…unless you're just messing with me."

"I'm not…

"Whatever. I'm through talking to you."

She turned to go and he grabbed her arm. "Don't rush off. Please? I really need to talk to you more. Give the viewers a good story. How about if you give me a kiss?" Color rose up the neck of his collar. "Just a small one."

"Are you crazy? Leave me alone. I don't know if you're faking this or not, but either way I don't want anything to do with you. If you have the bug, which I don't think you do, then you better look elsewhere for a partner, my friend." She removed his hand and pushed at the door. It didn't open, and she pushed harder.

Just then she felt a sharp pang in her bottom.

Her knees trembled, but she didn't look back. She felt her blood heat up, lust flow through her veins, and knew she had to get inside. Away from the bitten reporter, away from the bug that might have already found another innocent party to infect.

If it left a stinger, she'd get rid of it fast. No way in hell was she going to join the parade to the altar.

CHAPTER TWO

Mila locked the door behind her and bolted for the small restroom in the back of the store. She tugged her jeans down, and shifted her backside to get a look in the mirror. After scrutinizing her ass for several minutes, she finally noticed a small pink dot on one cheek.

Could be anything, she told herself. A pimple, a scratch. She'd only been imagining things. After all, it didn't hurt. Not like that poor reporter who seemed in some actual pain. And she didn't have a fever, either. Nope, she was fine, fine, fine.

She breathed a sigh of relief as she slipped her jeans back on, turned off the light, and went back to unlock the front door. Come on, customers! Bring in your bright smiles, your optimism, and your credit cards, and let Mila take care of the rest.

Strange what twists and turns had led her to this door. Growing up she certainly had never expected to be a wedding planner/buyer/shop keeper, and all the other labels she could attach to making her customers happy. Being a tom-boy at heart, she'd never been into girly things like Disney princesses or Barbie dolls or pretty dresses. Even as a teenager she hadn't engaged in gossipy girlfriends or crushing on boys. Romance was clearly not her thing. She was happier riding horses, skiing with her brothers, even mucking out a barn.

She'd begged her parents for a horse since she was about six years old and it was her doting, loving grandparents that gave her one for her thirteenth birthday. They offered to stable the young horse as long as she took sole care of him and continued to ride. She did this willingly with joy and with purpose. Every day after school she'd go to the stables and train with the thoroughbred she'd named, Lucky Lady. By the time she was sixteen she'd been quite a champ at show jumping—winning local competitions, lining her bedroom walls with ribbons and trophies. She'd loved the thrill of competition and being a horsewoman was all she wanted, until the summer she'd graduated high school and met a man she couldn't have.

John Turner had been a horse trainer and an accomplished jumper. Matter-of-fact he'd jumped more than just horses—he'd claimed her virginity by jumping her too. Happened in a stall on top of a pile of straw during an out-of-state competition. It hadn't been the most romantic place in the world for her first time ever, but it was all the romance she needed. She knew he was married, but that didn't stop her from loving him with her whole innocent heart. He'd promised he'd leave his wife and make everything all right, and she'd believed and trusted him, and one year drifted into the next. She'd tried to end things knowing it was wrong, but he always wooed her back. She'd been weak and clingy, and it hurt too much to let him go. It ended the way it began—with as much heat and passion and despair. When his pregnant wife found out, she'd taken great pleasure to drag both their names through the mud and the dung.

She'd been so ashamed that she couldn't face the horse people they knew. Soon after she sold Lucky Lady and stopped show jumping. It was a few years later that Nana and Poppa died and she'd never forgiven herself for letting them down.

Sheesh, why was she remembering this now? The affair had been almost six years ago, and she hadn't thought about him in a long, long time. This job kept her busy, and gave her no time to reflect on what ifs, or regrets of any kind. Besides, you couldn't go back and change the past, so you might as well forget about it, and move forward.

If she was still single, that was her choice. She liked the fact she wasn't a romanticist, just a sensible, hardworking business woman who knew how to take an opportunity when she saw it, and milk it for all it was worth. Besides, loving someone had made her weak and she'd never let that happen again. It had brought her nothing but pain and guilt and grief.

She stood near the windows of her shop watching the San Francisco reporter chatting with people, his crew filming it all. Everyone had an angle. His was selling a story. Hers was selling the fantasy of love.

She sighed. What would it be like to feel this crazy itch that brought her customers running to her store, eager to commit a lifetime together, knowing there was not even a hope of divorce? Shaking her head, she had to smile. The young couples were always head over heels in love. It was quite sweet really, and she wished a few of them would waltz in right about now. After all, she'd told the reporter how busy she was, and didn't want him writing something negative about Serendipity Falls, calling it a hoax. That might stop the influx of people moving in, and have an impact on her sales.

She folded her arms and tapped her toes. Waiting for customers was similar to watching an egg boil. And Mila was not one to sit around, she needed to keep active. As long as she had some time on her hands she might as well do an inventory, she told herself, and count the dresses she had in each size.

She fingered the silky satin and the creamy lace, and her heart hummed with pleasure. The dresses were so pretty and barely worn. Her dresses were all second hand but each precious gown had only lovingly been worn once. She purchased only designer gowns she found on-line, or hunted down in gently used boutiques around the Bay area. It was important to her that her brides-to-be had their special day too, even if the wedding was ridiculously rushed, and overpriced to accommodate the urgency.

Mila had handled all the arrangements for her brother, Devon and his fiancée Tara, because, well, she was better at it--it was her job after all, and both of them were too busy to take any interest in the details. They just wanted a simple wedding. Quick.

Their parents were flying in from Maui to attend the wedding, and they hadn't yet met their future daughter-in-law. It still blew her mind that her eldest brother was going to get married--and in such a rush, but who was she to complain? Tara would be the sister she never had, and she couldn't ask for a better friend or a better partner for her oldest brother. Devon and Tara both had tragedies in their past and deserved this happiness.

Tara was an executive pastry chef with the Cascade Resorts and chose to have her wedding in the beautiful garden area next to the pool. Darned if she wasn't making her own cake and the desserts for her wedding guests too. Beyond that, she had no interest in anything. Mila was to choose the floral arrangements, book a church official to preside over the ceremony, send out invitations and find her a suitable wedding dress.

She looked through her selection, imagining pretty Tara, with her long auburn hair, her sparkling green eyes, and her simple classic style. She would hate anything too elaborate or frilly. A sheath, perhaps off the shoulder or strapless would suit her best.

She pulled out a couple that she thought might do and decided to try them on as they were close to the same size. Taking the two dresses into the dressing room, she slipped out of her jeans and knit sweater, and slid on the strapless gown, loving the sexy and yet elegant style. She stood on tiptoe and glanced at herself in the mirror. The gown was gorgeous and she twirled around to see the back, just as the bells over the door alerted her to customers.

She hurried out of the dressing stall with an apologetic smile on her face. "Be right with you," she called, then saw it was the goofy reporter and his cameraman. "Oh, it's you."

His jaw opened, and his mouth opened and closed a few times. He was gaping at her like a love sick guppy. She'd seen that look on a few men in the past year, and it was enough to make her want to run and hide.

"You are stunning." Chase rushed forward and grabbed her two hands, pulling her deeper into the store. "Mike, take a picture. Our viewers will love this." His eyes were like hot coals as they raked over her. "Do you always model the dresses for your customers?"

"No," she sniffed, putting her nose in the air. "I'm not modeling. Just trying it on."

His eyes filled with concern. "Shit. You aren't getting married, are you?"

"No way. My soon to be sister-in-law asked me to keep an eye out for something she'd like."

"Well, if she looks anything like you, she's going to be one gorgeous bride."

"She will be, yes." Mila folded her arms, and fidgeted in her gown. "So, gentlemen, as you can see I don't have any customers yet. Why don't you walk around the mall some more, or go over to the restaurant next to the falls. You could find some people there to interview, and maybe even sample some of that spring water." She grinned. "If you're brave enough, that is."

"We're heading there later for lunch. Now that we're here why don't you show us around your shop?" Chase suggested. "We saw the boa and the champagne and picnic hamper in the window display, but I'm getting a different image inside." He turned to his crew. "What do you think, Mike? It certainly sets a mood. Somewhere between an upscale brothel and a romantic fantasy, wouldn't you say?"

"Brothel?" she gasped. "It does not!"

"Don't be annoyed. I wasn't meaning it in a derogatory way. Just, well, I was referring to the red velvet sofas and the heavy gold drapes. What do you think, Mike?"

"You're on your own with that one, buddy," Mike answered and walked away. Smart. Unlike roving reporter boy.

She smiled, and enjoyed his unease. "You're an expert on brothels, I see." She arched her brow. "Been in a few have you?"

"No. Can't say that I have." He picked up a lacy undergarment and raised a brow. "Nice. I like this."

"Put it down please, or do you have a lady friend you'd like to purchase it for?"

"Naw." He winked. "Hoped you'd do the honor and model it."

She rolled her eyes. "Are you always this annoying?"

"Not really, no." He gave a sheepish grin. "Seems you bring out the worst in me."

She took the black thong out of his hands and frowned. "Is that right? In that case, I suggest you leave." He was acting weird, and still had a flushed face and eyes like he was wired on something. If he was a druggie, she didn't want him in her store. Matter-of-fact, she didn't want him anyway.

"We'll only take a minute of your time." He glanced at his cameraman, as if seeking support. "We've only got a few days and the boss wants an exciting story. I hoped you might want to help us out."

"I'm sorry, but there's nothing much to show you. I do wedding invitations, sell consignment dresses, take orders for cakes, and that's about it. Well, I do have lingerie for the bride, and shoes to go with the dresses, elegant handbags, and a few aphrodisiacs on the counter near the cash register."

She pointed to a few things and felt her strapless gown dip a little. Unfortunately, she was rather well endowed and practically spilling out of the bustier. It would fit Tara perfectly, she decided. But, she needed to get out of it fast before she fell out. She gave it a hard tug upward.

Chase's eyes were drawn southward. "What else do you carry?" he stuttered. "Something erotic for the men?"

"No." Her spine straightened, which put her half exposed breasts further on display. She folded her arms over her chest, feeling ridiculous. "I have tuxes for rent, shirts, bow ties and cummerbunds, and small gifts that the groom could give his bride on their wedding night."

"This is starting to get interesting," he said with a glint in his eye. "What kind of gifts?"

She didn't answer right away. No way was she going to admit on camera about her secret stash of sexual favors. "As you can see this is a very specialized shop."

Mike was still walking around and snapping pictures. "What's this, behind the curtain?" he asked.

"It's nothing. Don't go in there."

He did anyway. "Well, well, well. I see we have some sex toys."

"Now we're getting somewhere." Chase grinned, moving forward to see her back room merchandise. "Get pictures of these," he told Mike and picked up one of her hottest sellers. "Good Gawd. How's a guy supposed to compete with that?"

She snatched the giant dildo out of his hands, and thrust herself in front of the display before the photographer could get his pictures. "I want you both to leave my store." She thrust out an arm. "Right now."

She could feel the back zipper sliding down, and knew it was a losing battle. If they didn't leave soon, they'd really get a photo moment. She hugged the bodice tight. "As you can see my customers haven't arrived yet. Please go wait outside until they do."

Chase stepped behind her and pulled her dress together, zipping it closed. His hands rested on her hips, the back of his fingers touching her bare flesh. She felt a surge of heat flow from his hands and light her entire body. Holy, Mother Mary. Every nerve end was on fire, eager for his touch.

She shoved him away from her, and fanned her face. "Oh, no, oh no. I'm burning up. What have you done? Did you bring that thing in with you?"

Chase's mouth dropped open. "Crap! Don't tell me you've got it too?" He backed away from her. "What's going on? How can we get rid of it?"

She threw up her hands. "You are going to stay away from me for starters. I'm not in lust, nor do I have any wish to be. Go and please don't ever come back into this shop again." She gave him a push, and kept moving him toward the door. "Both of you, out!"

Chase was halfway out the door, when he turned to look at her. She felt seared from head to toe. "I'll try to stay away, but I can't promise." He gave her a heated look that nearly melted her panties off, if she'd been wearing any. "I'd high-tail it out of town but I'm in need of a story. Besides, you'd miss me if I left…"

"Go to hell and take that bug, or whatever, with you."

CHAPTER THREE

Chase left the store, ignoring Mike. He hadn't been kidding. His insides were in turmoil and the blood in his veins ran hot. He wanted to go back into that store, rip that bodice right off of her, and do her every which way but Sunday. He'd never felt such lust before. Sure, he liked women a lot, and had his share of them too, but this was primal. It wasn't a want, but a must have. One way or the other, Mila was his. He just had to figure out a way to get her in his bed and the sooner the better.

Mike nudged his arm. "Hey, lover boy. Wake up. You look a little punchy, right about now. You really think you got bitten or were you messing around back there?"

"I don't know what happened," he stammered.

"Make a hell of a story. You could be the hero of your own piece, my friend." Mike laughed so hard he began to gasp. "Shit man, this is fucking great."

Chase shook his head, trying to clear the image of Mila, naked, withering under him. Her scent lingered on his mind, the feel of her flesh when he touched her bare back. He'd felt her shiver and knew she wanted him too. They had to have each other. At least once.

His mind was reeling. How could he ditch his cameraman and get pretty Mila where she needed to be?

"So what are you going to do about it?" Mike asked.

"I'm not sure." He ran a hand through his hair, feeling about as frustrated as some horny kid with his first Playboy magazine. "Why don't you go to the falls and I'll catch up?"

"Like hell you will. You wanna go back inside there, don't you?" Mike snickered. "Good luck. She's a spit-fire, that one."

"Shut the hell up," Chase snapped. "Don't talk about her. Okay?" He shuddered, breaking into a cold sweat. "You're not the one who got bit. What the frig am I going to do? She doesn't want anything to do with me, and I sure don't want to get married. I've got a lot of living yet to do." He rammed his hands in his jean pockets. "I'm only twenty-eight. Shit, shit, shit."

"You should have thought about that before volunteering for this story." Mike stopped grinning, and gave him a worried look. "You really look bad. Like you're burning up with a fever. God damn. Hope the bloody thing isn't catchy. I'm a married man and want to stay that way."

"Don't blame you. Maybe I should give the boss a call," Chase suggested. "Tell him we've got to come back early. Say the story doesn't check out or something."

"Good idea. We could be home in time for dinner."

Chase called but Jason, the senior editor, insisted they stay overnight and do a little more digging. "You're not the first reporters to try to uncover the truth. Something is definitely going on up there and I want you to find out what. Don't come back until you do."

"I think we're wasting our time, but hey, it's your money. You want us to hang out here and see if we can find some love bug—no problem." Chase sucked in a deep breath. What if he had been bit? Would it work itself out of his system, or would he be lusting after a woman he didn't even want? Well, he wanted to get between her legs, but that wasn't the same as wanting to spend an eternity together.

"A couple of days," Jason said. "There's something to this story. I can feel it."

"You got it, boss." A few days, a few nights. Pleasurable, lust filled nights he hoped. He could handle that, then skedaddle home, back to his bachelor pad. He rented a one bedroom apartment a block from Ocean Beach and spent his free time surfing or just chilling out. The proximity to the city made this location practical, but the ocean was his life's blood. Couldn't imagine living anywhere else—unless he was on assignment, covering some news worthy event. Not like this one. How did he end up here—reporting about a wedding fever and a ridiculous love bug in the spring water? Perhaps he shouldn't have dated the boss's daughter after all.

This was his revenge. Sending him off to the mountains, perhaps hoping he might succumb to the mysterious forces that drove innocent men and women to a binding marriage. Hell. Shoot me now. He hadn't seen it coming, but that's exactly what Jason wanted—to keep him here long enough that he would leave his daughter alone.

Well, that was not going to happen. Besides, they'd broken up a few months ago. Didn't she tell her father anything? Obviously not. Now he was stuck here in the mountains for a few days, and already he'd come down with a fever.

A fever and an itch. He shivered, feeling a sudden cold. If he were to stay a few more days he'd darn well need something hot to warm him up.

Mila's face flitted to mind. He instantly stiffened and his jeans got tight. His head wasn't interested, but his body was reacting in ways that were hard to ignore. Perhaps one night wrapped around the luscious Mila might cure him of this love bug crap. And if not, it'd certainly make his fever more bearable. And he'd have an open-ended story for his boss, the outcome yet to be decided.

"Okay, Mike. I have one or two things to do here to wrap things up, so why don't you go on ahead of me? We'll grab lunch at the falls," he glanced at his watch, "say in half an hour?"

"What do you have to do?" Mike said suspiciously.

"I need a haircut and there's always good gossip in the salons." He ran a hand through his hair.

Mike gave him a long look. "You don't sound as crazed as you did in that store, but still I'm worried. If you've got it, keep it to yourself. Don't infect me, okay?" Mike put his camera away in his equipment bag, and stuck it over his shoulder. "One more thing. Leave that girl alone. Last thing we need is a rape charge."

Chase's fingers curled into a fist. "I've never raped a woman in my life. And you don't need to worry on my account. No woman is going to distract me from getting this story, and getting the hell away from here." He lifted his chin. "I hear the sound of the surf calling me and a wave with my name on it."

Chase waited until Mike disappeared, then he hustled back to Wedding Fever, ignoring the warning from his pal and the one in his gut.

Mila glanced up from whatever she was doing, and frowned. "You. I told you not to come back."

He took three giant steps and reached her side. He took hold of her shoulders and pulled her close. Her eyes were wide, but not frightened. Her luscious mouth popped open. She licked her lips, and shook her head. "No."

"Yes." His arms encircled her waist, and his mouth grazed her neck. He breathed in her scent and felt dizzy with relief. She was an aphrodisiac that he couldn't resist. "I'm sorry. I have to. Just once." She didn't ask what, so he tilted her head and claimed her mouth.

Mila didn't push away, but seemed frozen, accepting his kiss but not giving anything in return. Kissing her was enough to satisfy him for a moment or two, but then he had to have more. The sweetness of her lips was like honey to a bee.

"Mila?" His heart pounded and so did hers.

He pried her mouth open, and slipped in his tongue, needing to taste her, craving more of her sweetness, savoring the very essence of her. If he had died, then this was heaven.

She pushed at his chest, trying to break free, but he continued to kiss her as though he could not breathe without her.

After a second or two more she gasped, then grabbed on to his lapels and sucked the breath right out of him. Oh, Lordy. He didn't know why he'd come back in, except to get rid of this hurtful, urgent, physical need, but instead of assuaging his desire, it stroked the fire.

He broke away first. Her eyes were dewy and soft, her lips wet and full. Her chest heaved, and he could feel her hardened nipples and knew they ached to be touched.

He groaned and ran a hand through his hair. He wanted to do her so bad, but he had to stop before he had her naked on the floor. He sucked in a few painful breaths, his eyes never breaking contact with hers. The pupils were dark and dilated, two enormous moons in her beautiful vibrant face. She was aglow, lit from within.

The love bug had found them both and he didn't have a fucking clue what to do about it, but he'd figure it out one day at a time. Getting her into his bed was his short term goal. His one and only plan. He couldn't think beyond that.

"I'm staying here tonight," he panted. "I'll be at the Fairmont. I'd like to see you there."

She shivered and straightened up. She put a hand on her heaving chest. Sucked in some air, and released it slowly. She was trembling, and he wanted to hold her close and make the tremors stop.

He reached for her but she stepped away. "No."

"Why not? You're shaking. I want to comfort you."

"Comfort me?" She tilted her head up, and locked eyes with him. "You just forced yourself on me. I should call the cops."

She was trying to be cool, but he wasn't buying it. "You should call the fire department to put out this flame between us."

Her lips curved into a smug smile. "Who said I felt anything? Just because you're acting crazy and have got it bad, doesn't mean I feel the same. Trust me, I don't. I enjoyed the kiss as much as the next girl, but I'm certainly not lusting after you and I don't intend to get married. Not for years. I'm having way too much fun as it is. So you can just go away and find someone else to fall in love with."

"Maybe I will." His eyes dropped to her mouth, and he tugged her closer. "After one last kiss."

She turned her head. "I'll count to three, then you better not be here."

He kissed her cheek, and nibbled on the long, slender neck she'd exposed. His teeth grazed her ear, and she flinched. "Your loss," he whispered. "And mine."

"Out!"

"I'll be waiting for you." He entwined his fingers with hers. "Tonight."

"Don't lose any sleep over me." She pulled her hand away. "I won't be coming."

"Oh, yes you will. In more ways than one." With that, he left.

He didn't know how his feet carried him since his legs had turned to mush, but somehow he managed to find the salon, get his hair trimmed, and get to the falls before Mike became suspicious.

CUPID

I'd been sitting among the tray of aphrodisiacs when the young reporter and his cameraman walked in, and shame on me, but I had a mouth full of chocolate. Oh, the terrible fright I had when the man with the camera began walking around and snapping pictures! I was so worried that he might catch me on film and then the whole world would come running to Serendipity Falls and I would become a major celebrity. I might want respect as much as the next person, but I don't want to be fussed over like the guy who used to wear a glittery glove, or that boy Beiber. No, I'm not exactly shy, but more of a private person, Cupid, whatever. So I quickly snuck between the dark chocolate and a ripe avocado and landed on a fig.

Not enough humans know about the pleasures of aphrodisiacs, and I'd be amiss if I didn't mention this now. Take chocolate for example. It has two special ingredients, both made for love. The one is a feel good chemical and the other, PEA releases dopamine in the pleasure center of the brain which, they say, peaks during orgasms. Yes, and there's more good news. This PEA also induces feelings of excitement, attraction and euphoria. So, not only does it taste good—it's good for your sex life too.

Another lovely aphrodisiac is a fig. Did you know that opened it emulates the female sex organ and is historically linked to love and fertility? Ah, yes. See the things a Cupid knows. Another interesting tidbit that I must share--Aztecs referred to avocados as a testicle tree! It's all about the shape, my dears. Here's some more gossip for you--Catholic priests in Spain once forbade this obscenely sexual fruit.

So there you have it. Direct from the Cupid's mouth. Not that I'm bragging, but I'm quite the expert on love, you know.

Now, what was I saying before I went on and on about aphrodisiacs? Oh, yes, after the men left, I took a little nap, and opened my eyes when I heard the doorbell tinkle. I peeked behind a fig and saw the young man Chase had returned alone to the shop where the pretty lady waited. Let me tell you--it did my heart wonders when I saw the warmth of their kiss.

These two young people would be so good for each other. That poor dear, little Mila had such a bad experience with her first love that she'd never wanted to chance her heart again. Such a shame, really. There is no joy in the world without love, and so many humans don't realize that fact. Oh, they fill their days with work and play, minor diversions to help them escape the true meaning in life.

Love is all we need. Who said that? It was a bug of some kind, wasn't it? Yes, I remember now, it was a beetle.

Well, the beetle said it best. All we need is love. Without it we are nothing but a protective shell. A tortoise afraid to stick out our heads in case something bad happens. Heck, I'm only a Cupid, but I know that is no way to live.

Life is full of chances and choices that can lead down many paths, but unless you're willing to take one and see where it may lead, you will never know the freedom and joy that the world can unfold.

I witnessed the expression on Mila's face as she returned the kiss from that boy, Chase. The wonder, the promise, the excitement had lit up her face and ignited a flame which had been put out so many years before.

Open your heart, dear children. Follow the path and riches will be yours.

CHAPTER FOUR

The second Chase left, Mila rushed back into the changing room, stripped off the gown, and slipped back into her clothes. Her fingers were trembling, and her chest heaved. Why had he kissed her? And why had she kissed him back?

Dammit, didn't she know enough about all this crazy romantic stuff to stay the hell clear? She should never, ever have kissed him. Now she wanted him. Bad. She craved him, and she'd never craved anyone in her entire adult life. Well, except John Turner, that married two-timing jerk, but that was a long, long time ago. When she'd been young and stupid. Now she was just stupid.

She splashed her face with cold water, took several deep breaths, fighting the desire that curled inside her belly, heated her loins, and made her weak. Whatever he had done to her, she had to undo it. Now, before it grew tentacles that wrapped around her heart. She had to break free, shake it off and refuse to be a victim. She sold romance, she didn't buy it.

After several minutes, her insides quieted, the fever subsided, but still her skin remained clammy and cold.

Her butt cheek was sore too. Must be a mosquito bite but how did a mosquito get inside the mall? Damn. Everything was so irritating.

To keep her mind from Chase, the kiss, and the Fairmont hotel, she busied herself with the jobs still at hand. Flowers to order for one bride, a cake for another, wedding invitations to get out, favors for guests, and dresses for the bridesmaids, plus there was a bachelor party she had to plan for next week. So much to organize in such a limited time, but then that was her life. She took care of every small detail so the bride and groom wouldn't have to worry about a thing.

Before closing she'd had another two brides show up within minutes of each other, both demanding that they must be married on the same day. She'd had to break up a cat fight and promise that she would find different locations for both weddings and receptions, and insisted she could handle the rest.

"It's what I do," she told both young women, handing them tissues to mop up their tears. "I've been in this business for the past five years, and I have never disappointed anyone in the past. You can go online and see the reviews. Not one person has ever had a bad word to say, and I aim to keep it that way."

She poured them both a glass of champagne and brought out a small dish of caviar, and by the time the girls left they were new best friends. Mila kicked off her shoes and sat down to finish the rest of the champagne and caviar, knowing it would be dinner. Then she shuffled the few blocks home, tired to the bone from her emotionally exhausting day.

After a long, hot shower she poured a cup of tea and sat down to read a book, but then Tara called to say she had a free dinner for two at the Fairmont, and would she please join her?

"I know it's a drive, but it won't take you long," Tara said. "Please? Devon's at the bar and I don't want to eat alone."

"I'm frazzled from work, and was settling in for the night. Can we push it off until tomorrow?"

"No. Wish we could, but I got a call this afternoon inviting me and a guest to come by and sample the menu I chose for our rehearsal dinner. Not that we are rehearsing, but it's a chance for our families to meet before the wedding."

"I know, and it's wonderful. But I really don't want to drive to the Fairmont tonight. Sorry."

"Take a cab. I'll pay for it." Tara lowered her voice, "Pretty please? I don't have anyone else to ask."

"I had an extremely exhausting day." Mila yawned, hoping that would end matters. "If it were here that would be fine, but going all the way up to Mammoth? I'd really prefer not to."

"Get your ass up here, dear matron of honor." Tara rushed on, "There's more news reporters doing a story on Serendipity Falls. I mean, how cool is that? There's going to be a major explosion, which will be good for both our businesses."

Tara had recently put an offer in for a bed and breakfast joint that was seriously run-down but in a great tourist spot, with a view of the emerald lake and falls. If the offer was accepted, she hoped to have it renovated and up and running by the following year.

"Yeah, I met them already. They interviewed me and some others at the mall this morning."

"Oh, right. Of course they did. Maybe you'll be on the six o'clock news. Turn it on."

She clicked on the TV set, hoping like hell that she wouldn't be seen wearing the wedding dress. Especially when she'd already hand picked it for Tara.

"Forget the news. I'll do my matronly duties and get my ass of the couch. See you in about forty-five."

"Good. And speaking of news, I've got some for you too." Tara giggled and then hung up.

Mila walked into her closet and pulled out some clothes. Now what? Hadn't she had enough surprises in one day? Then a thought struck her. Maybe Tara was pregnant—that had to be it. She'd be an aunt and could spoil the little darling as much as she wanted, without having to deal with the consequences.

She tugged on some tight leather black pants, a clingy top, a pair of high heeled boots, then reapplied her make-up, brushed out her long dark hair, and tried not to think about who she might run into at the hotel. If she did happen to see Chase, she would do her best to discourage him, but kindly of course. After all, it wasn't his fault he'd been infected, and that she was the object of his desire. She was the only woman in sight when it happened. It wasn't personal.

And the very last thing she wanted was to meet up with him and make this impersonal connection, personal.

An hour later Mila waltzed into the lobby and spotted Tara talking with a great looking guy. They were both laughing and seemed on very friendly terms. Mila frowned, not liking the idea of this fellow smiling so fondly at her soon-to-be-sister-in-law.

Tara turned her head, saw her standing near the door, and waved her over.

"Mila, I'd like you to meet Ty Jamison. He's a contractor and we were discussing plans for my B&B." She grinned and punched fists in the air. "Yes. I got it. Signed the papers today."

"Oh." Mila felt a moment's relief, quickly followed by disappointment. "So you're not pregnant?"

"No, silly, is that what you thought?"

She nodded. "Yeah. Kind of got my hopes up, but hey, congratulations. The Bed and Breakfast will be your baby too."

She shook hands with Ty, wishing Tara's contractor wasn't quite so attractive since they would be working closely together. Not as handsome as Devon, but still a little too appealing, and with an air about him that told Mila he knew it. "Hi. I'm Mila. So you'll be working with Tara? Fixing up the old B&B." She glanced at Tara. "How did you find someone so quick?"

Ty answered. "I've done a lot of local work and my reputation speaks for itself." He shrugged his impressive shoulders. "I was the first person on her list."

Tara nodded. "Called him about ten minutes after I sealed the deal. I wanted to make sure he could do my renovations since he's the best contractor around."

"I'm sure we'll create something really great together," he replied.

Mila bristled, going into protective mode. This was her brother's future bride, and not just anyone he was flirting with. "I found the perfect wedding dress for you," she said to Tara, giving Ty a pointed look. "She's marrying my brother in two weeks."

"I heard. Congratulations. He's a lucky guy." He smiled and glanced at Mila. "Tara was telling me about your shop in town. Doing a lively business, I hear."

"Can't complain. And now that we have news reporters spreading the word, things should pick up even more this summer. Normally it's our slow season, but I've got a good feeling not this year. Our real estate market has already taken off."

"I know. I'm doing a little speculating as well."

"Would you like to join us for a drink?" Tara asked him. "We're having our rehearsal dinner here and Mila and I are here for a complimentary tasting."

"Thanks for the offer but I won't keep you." He nodded at Mila. "Pleasure meeting you. I'm sure I'll be seeing you around."

She nodded. "I'm not hard to find."

The girls watched him leave, both taking in his tight butt and pressed jeans. "I thought you might like him," Tara said with a smile. "It's time you found someone special too."

"You wanted me to meet him?" She looked at Tara, and felt badly for doubting her even for a second. "I'm sorry, I should have been nicer, but I thought he was interested in you."

"Heck no. I only met him a couple of hours ago, but he came highly recommended." She smiled. "When I saw how handsome he was, I thought of you." She put an arm around Mila's waist and gave her a hug. "I want you to be as happy as I am."

"No way," Mila made a face. "I'm too busy. Besides it's more fun selling romance, than losing my head over some guy. For me, anyway."

"I felt the same way not so long ago." Taking Mila's arm, she led her toward the dining room. "Hard to believe it's already May. Seems like I just moved here yesterday."

"And yet so much has happened. You and Devon fell in love. He nearly died in that avalanche, and you never left his side. Now you're two weeks away from being Mrs. O'Reilley."

"I like the sound of that. I really do." Tara toyed with the engagement ring on her finger, and the one carat diamond sparkled as brightly as her smile.

"We need to drink to the love bug or whatever brought you two together."

"Yes, we should. I'm so very fortunate. Serendipity Falls is truly a magical place, and I agree with Dev about mountain living. It's a tight community and I feel like I've come home. I never want to leave it."

"Aren't you going to Maui for a honeymoon?" Mila grinned. "If you're not using your tickets, maybe I could?"

"Ha, ha, ha. Very funny." Tara added, "I'm so looking forward to meeting your mom and dad. We've skyped a few times and I know that I'm going to love them."

"And they, you."

Tara gave her name to the maitre d' and they were escorted to their table. They ordered a Chardonnay and sat and chatted while each course was presented.

They picked away at their delicious endive salad with pear and caramelized pecans, then ordered a glass of Napa Valley's finest Pinot to accompany the beautifully prepared Beef Wellington. Although every bite was scrumptious they had to leave room for a taste of the apple strudel dessert. The chef came out between each course, asking if everything was prepared to their tastes.

Since Tara was an executive pastry chef at the Cascade resort, the chef probably wondered why she'd chosen the Fairmont to host the wedding party dinner. Mila knew that Tara had wanted a different location from her wedding, something romantic and intimate. They were dining in an alcove next to the wall of windows with a view of the outdoor pool and gardens, a lovely setting for a table of sixteen.

Tara's mother had died young, and she'd only recently met her father's new wife. The two of them would be attending the wedding and Mila's parents were flying in from Hawaii. Then there was Kyle, her younger brother and his girlfriend, Devon's best man Josh and his date. Mila, the maid of honor, would be the only one single at the table.

Maybe she could invite Ty, since he'd make a nice accessory on her arm. She could just imagine him all decked out in a tux, and knew that in or out of it he'd be an attractive sight.

"What are you smiling about?" Tara asked.

"Eye candy. I should bring someone to your wedding, and wondered if Ty might be interested. I could use a dance partner."

"You could use someone for a whole lot more than that. You know what they say about all work and no play." She gave Mila a brief hug. "I'll give you his number and be sure to use it. I'm sure he'll be delighted. His eyes certainly lit up when he looked at you."

"I doubt that, but we'll see. I could use a little diversion right now."

"Oh, and why is that? Some problems at work?"

"I'll tell you on the way out." They got up from the table, popped in to thank the chef, then left the dining room and found a sofa in the lobby where they could sit and talk a little longer.

Mila was about to give Tara an edited version of what happened earlier today, when a familiar voice made her turn her head.

"You came." Chase stood behind her, grinning like an idiot, his arms held wide.

"I did not," she replied, shooting Tara a horrified glance. She could feel her cheeks flush hot.

Tara saw the blush and looked amused. "And who might you be?" she asked in a playful voice.

"Chase Carlton of the San Francisco News." He held out his hand. "Are you the one getting married soon? Mila was modeling a gown for me and my cameraman."

"I was not." Mila folded her arms, and gave Chase an angry look. "I was just checking out the size to see if it would fit you," she told Tara.

"She looked amazing in it. I'm sure you will too."

"Oh, shut up," Mila snapped. "I was falling out of the dress and you know it."

"Didn't bother me at all," he said, and gave Tara an apologetic smile. "Is she always this testy? I can't seem to say anything right."

"You could say good-bye," Mila told him.

"I'm not going anywhere. I'm staying here, remember?"

"Not for long, I hope."

"As long as it takes. My boss has told me to find out what's going on in this place, and until I do he wants me to stay."

"You can't stay," Mila stammered. "It's not healthy."

Tara looked from one to the other. "Oh, oh."

Mila's eyes narrowed and she shook her head in denial. "Oh, oh, what? Don't even think it, Tara. I'm warning you."

"Don't tell me. You've got it."

"No, I haven't. Nor does he." Her eyes flew to Chase's face, and she felt something really scary flare up inside. She was ice cold with fear, but felt a liquid warmth flood her being. Like molten lava it spread up her legs, into her cervix, her tummy, her chest, and threatened to suffocate her. She breathed deeply, forcing air around the constriction. "We have nothing, right, Chase? Tell her."

"Well, I'm not so sure about that." Chase rubbed his jaw. "Haven't stopped thinking about you all day, and that kiss was damn hot."

"Kiss?" Tara's eyes and mouth popped open. "You've already kissed?"

"No!" Mila denied it, not wanting it to be true. "He attacked me, and I allowed it, I suppose." She couldn't meet Chase's eyes, and hung her head in shame.

"Attacked nothing. You were into it as much as me." He touched Mila's bowed head. "You don't have to be afraid. I'm not here to disrupt your life. Hell, I don't want that either."

"Oh shut up, and go away. I came here to be with Tara, not with you."

"Deny as much as you want, but yet, here you are." He lifted her chin so she'd be forced to look at him. "There's plenty of hotels and bars in this village, but you showed up at the one you knew I was staying. You wanted to see me, all right."

Tara stood up. She shook hands with Chase. "Nice to meet you, but I think I'll let the two of you figure this out on your own." She smiled at Mila. "You do need a date, and why not?"

Mila's mouth opened and then clamped shut. She shook her head. Tears sprang to her eyes and she never cried. At least not since her Grams and Papa died, but she'd loved them so very much and they'd died so tragically. This was not tragic. This was merely irritating. "I can't believe you're ditching me like this," she snapped. "How could you, Tara? I don't want to be left alone with him."

Tara bent over and kissed her cheek. "I love you. You know that. But I honestly think this might turn into something wonderful, and I don't want to be in the middle of it. Good luck to you both."

Mila watched her waltz away, and silently she called her every name in the book. Traitor, was just one of them. The others were worse.

"What did she mean by that?" Chase asked and sat down on the sofa next to her. He took her hand and intertwined his fingers with hers. It was an intimate gesture considering they'd only just met.

She glanced at their joined hands and felt almost resigned. Her head hurt, and her stomach was doing a circus act. "She thinks the bug got us. We're doomed."

CHAPTER FIVE

Chase dropped her hand as if a scorpion had bit him, then slowly, carefully picked it up again. "I'm not convinced this thing is real, but something is not right. I mean I'm attracted to you and all that, but I sure don't want to get married. I only asked you to join me, thinking we could maybe do something about this attraction. You know—hook up for a night or two. No harm in that since I'm only here for a few days."

"That's what you thought? That I'd be easy and agree to sleep with you?"

"I was hoping you might. Figured that since we're both lusting after each other, we might as well give in and get it while it's good. Then we'll go our separate ways and never think about each other again." He glanced at her, putting on a shame-faced smile. "So what do you think?"

"I think you're certifiable and I have no idea why the news station allows you to go around representing them. Do they have any inkling as to how you behave?"

"I've never propositioned anyone like this before, so probably not. It's just different with you. This attraction I mean. It's kinda wild. Sexy. Hot. Maybe it is the love bug, right?" He leaned over and kissed her neck. "I can get a hellova story. First hand knowledge and all that."

"I'm not going to part of your story, or an accessory to your lust." She stood up. "I'm sorry if I gave you the wrong impression, but I have to be leaving now. I don't do what you want me to do with strange men. And you certainly classify as strange."

"Not if you got to know me, which you could. We could spend hours getting to know each other. We could talk, make love. Besides, it's getting late and you don't want to be driving down the mountain this time of night. What if you had an emergency or something?"

"I've lived here most of my life, so I think I can handle myself in the dark. Preferably alone."

"You handle yourself in the dark?" The erotic image shot right through him, lighting up all those dark places where his mind should fear to go. "I could help you out with that."

"You're disgusting, ya know that?"

He chuckled. "Didn't mean to go there, but hell. Couldn't help myself." He stepped closer to her and whispered in her ear. "What I was going to suggest was since you're already here and I have a very nice room upstairs with a king size bed, that perhaps you could spend the night with me and drive down in the morning."

"You want me to dive down where in the morning?"

"Drive, not dive, although that is an appealing thought." He looked at her closely, wondering why he just couldn't behave. She certainly brought out the worst in him.

"I don't think so, but thanks for asking. It's not often I get such a delightful request." She smiled sweetly, and that was just too much. He had to taste her now or die trying.

"Don't say no. How can I convince you to stay?" Before she could slip away he put his arms around her back, effectively trapping her, and guided her forward. His mouth captured hers in one hot fast kiss. Her breath was delicious, her warm mouth an appetizer that made him drool.

She, on the other hand, seemed to have a difference of opinion, if the fact she was beating his chest with her tiny fists meant anything.

He let her go, but not without regret. "You don't like me?"

She shook her head. "No, it's got nothing to do with you personally. It's just…well…this is the crazy stuff that happens around here, and I don't want any part of it. If you had any sense, you'd high tail it out of here as fast as you can."

"You make me want to stay. I know I should be afraid, but I'm not." His eyes dropped to her mouth. He liked watching her lips, almost as much as he enjoyed kissing them.

"That's not good." She gnawed her bottom lip, driving him crazy.

He shifted his stance, trying to ease the itch between his legs. "Can I at least walk you to your car?"

"Yes. That will be fine. But no funny stuff, okay? I don't want to hurt you, and I'm a kick boxer and master Karate."

"Ouch—that's sounds serious."

"It is. Keeps me in shape, and gives me the confidence to know that I can handle myself."

"There you go again. Always handling yourself," he said with a smile.

"There you go again—mind in the gutter."

"You should let yours go too. Just for one night. Come on. We're both adults and we're attracted to each other." He lifted a finger to stroke her cheek. "Besides, think of the fun we could have."

"I'd rather not. I've seen too much of this good thing around here and you can't toy with it. You have to take it seriously. If you don't, you're a goner. I've seen it time and time again and I have way too much common sense to allow it to happen to me."

"What are you running away from?"

"You for starters."

"I'm not the kick boxer." He put an arm around her back leading her toward the doors. "You better get home, beautiful Mila. Don't want you catching heaven knows what."

She nodded and he followed her out, allowing her to lead the way. They kept in step but didn't say anything more. When she got within twenty feet of her Range Rover, she turned and thanked him for seeing her safely to the car.

"I'll wait until you back out." He hated his gentlemanly manners, and wished he could go with his gut and ravish her. But he wasn't brought up that way. When a lady said no, it meant no, even if she really meant yes.

"Okay." She gave him a small smile. "Good luck with your story."

"You stay safe, you hear."

She slid into the Range Rover, and turned the key. Nothing happened. Tried again. Not a peep from the engine.

Chase stepped forward, and his hopes flared. "Want me to try?"

She gave him a worried look. "Dammit! This has never happened before. You don't think fate's playing a wicked game with us, do you?"

"Hell if I know. Step out and let see."

She did as he said, and he slipped into the driver's seat. After a couple of failed attempts, he jumped out and couldn't help but grin. "Looks like you've got a dead battery, young lady."

"Figured that." She sighed, and tucked her hands in her pockets. "What rotten luck. Least I've got AAA."

"You want to give them a call?"

She nodded and looked near tears.

"Hey, don't get upset. We'll take care of it."

"Okay." She sniffed. "I just wish I hadn't come out tonight. I've got a bad feeling about this. Like we're being messed with."

"No way," he scoffed. "Just a dead battery. Could happen to anyone." He tucked his hand through her arm. "Let's go back inside and call from my room. Might as well be comfortable while we wait."

She hesitated, and probably for good reason. He didn't intend to do anything she didn't want, but what if she wanted the same thing he did? Then it was fair game. Right?

She locked her car and they returned to the hotel lobby, heading for the bank of elevators that would lead them upstairs. The door slid open and he stepped in. She stood, looking at the empty elevator reluctantly.

He raised a brow. "You coming or staying?"

"Will you behave?"

"Always." His eyes held hers hoping he could convince her. He really didn't want to take advantage of her. He wanted to help her and let her see that he was a nice guy. If she wanted to spend the night, he could sleep on the chair. Didn't get much nicer than that.

She stepped in and he kept his distance as the elevator rose to the sixth floor. They got off and she walked slowly behind him down the long corridor.

He slid his key in, held the door for her to go through.

She stood at the threshold and he reached around her to flick on a light. When he faced her once more, she'd lost some of her keep-back attitude. There was a slight relaxation of her shoulders, a softening of her mouth.

"Don't be nervous." A sudden roll of his stomach made him realize he was giving bad advice. He wiped clammy palms against his jeans, wishing he hadn't invited her to his room after all. Logic pierced his lust-fogged brain, warning him something about this was not right. The dead battery--her showing up just as he planned to turn in for the night. Too circumstantial. Fate might be messing with them after all. It took every well-mannered bone in his body to keep from slamming the door in her face.

"I'm not afraid." She pushed past him, as if to prove it.

Self-protective instincts kicked into gear. He turned on the bedside lights, making sure to give her plenty of space. "Go ahead. Make your call." Sex with her was not just sex – in Serendipity Falls it was marriage and family and good-bye surfing.

She picked up her cell phone and was about to punch in the number. Instead, she dropped it back into her handbag. "Can I use your restroom?"

"Sure, but don't be long. It's getting late and I don't like the idea of you driving down the mountain alone."

He turned on the TV while she went inside and flicked at the channels. She was taking her time, and his guts were in knots. Inviting her back to the room hadn't been such a good idea after all.

When she came back out, she'd brushed her hair, reapplied her lipstick and unbuttoned her jacket. She was wearing those leather pants and a thin sweater that outlined every damn curve.

He swallowed hard and a nerve pulsed in his throat. She had a glitter in her eye, and he didn't like the way she moved toward him. All of a sudden she looked like the hunter with him as her chosen prey.

CHAPTER SIX

Mila shrugged out of her leather jacket and dropped it to the floor. "I don't feel like leaving quite yet," she said, weaving her way seductively around the bed.

"You need to call AAA. Right now. You shouldn't be hanging around here," he answered.

"Do you have anything to drink? I'm extremely thirsty and I feel hot. Very hot." She licked her lips and fanned her chest, smiling as his eyes dropped to her breasts.

"There's water in the bar under the counter."

She bent over, reaching for the water, knowing it gave him a view of her ass.

"Can I make the call for you?"

She opened the bottle and poured the cold liquid down her throat. With her head thrown back her breasts swelled under the thin knit shirt. She could feel her nipples hardening and a tingling in her female parts.

"You trying to get rid of me?" She wiped her mouth with the back of her hand, and let her eyes wander over him. She couldn't miss the fact his jeans were stretched to the breaking point and knew he wanted sex as much as she did.

He looked worried, and he should be. During the short elevator ride common sense had fled and primal need took over. The close proximity in that small enclosed space had heightened her senses and made every nerve end tingle. She'd been instantly aware of everything, from the slight scent of his aftershave to the fabric softener in his clothes. She'd wanted to lick him all over, taste, touch and feel.

Escaping to the bathroom, she'd hoped to distract herself long enough to regain a certain amount of control. Didn't happen. Her entire body felt charged, like an Energizer battery. Lust overrode any attempt at common sense.

"What's gotten into you?" He stood up and moved restlessly about the room.

"Nothing." She shrugged, and licked her lips. She hadn't been this turned on since – never. Everything she looked at was through a lens of desire. "Or maybe it's not nothing. Might be that Serendipity bug got me after all." She laughed again, the sound huskier than normal. "It's crazy, isn't it?"

"This really isn't a good idea." He backed the chair he sat in against the wall. "I'm sure you'll feel differently about it tomorrow. My suggestion is that you go home, or at least go to bed and sleep it off. I'm not going to touch you like this. You'll regret it, and so will I."

Regret? She waved the idea away, caught up by a surge of need. "You won't regret it. I promise." Before he could respond, she moved quickly and sat on his lap. She took his face into her hands and kissed him deeply. He stirred beneath her.

"There," she said with some satisfaction. "That doesn't feel so terrible, does it?"

"Get off me," he said in a strangled whisper.

She licked his neck in answer, and nipped on his ear. "You don't want me to go, any more than I do." Warm feelings flowed through her, feelings that she had thought had died in her years ago.

"I am not going to take advantage of you in this condition."

"What condition? I'm not drunk." She ran her fingers through his hair and kissed him lightly on the mouth. "I know perfectly well what I'm doing. I'm seducing you." She looked into his dreamy blue eyes and felt a yearning deep in her soul. As deep and as fathomless as the emerald lake below the falls.

"Well, just stop. Okay? Let's think about this."

She wanted him too much to stop. She wasn't promiscuous, and besides her married boyfriend she could count the number of men she'd dated and slept with. There had been three.

She got horny once in a while, or lonely, and would find someone to spend some time with but she didn't let her heart get involved. Not since John played her for a fool. She'd trusted him and believed that he'd leave his wife for her, but he'd only been dicking around.

The men she slept with now, well, it was done on her terms.

"Relax. Go with the flow," she told him and kissed him again. She pried his lips open with her tongue and moved around on top of him. She could feel the length of him, the heat building between him and her. She enjoyed the heat, the excitement, this strange desire. So long since she'd wanted a man—and it had never been as powerful as this.

"We said we'd wait." His hips lifted so she'd have better access. "No sex."

"What we are feeling is natural, mutual. We aren't hurting anyone. Feels pretty damn good, actually. What's the matter?" She kissed her way down his neck. Not understanding her raging pheromones, and at the moment beyond caring.

He took her hand and put it on his crotch. "Trying to be the voice of reason here, and failing." He ground his mouth to hers and she clung to him. "I don't want you blaming me in the morning."

Ravenous with desire, Mila gave into the feelings, her body on fire. She couldn't get close enough to him, learning the shape of his brow, the bridge of his nose, his strong jaw by touch. The taste of his mouth, the texture of his skin was new, exciting, sinfully delicious. "Nobody's fault," she murmured, kissing him everywhere at once.

His hand crept under her ass, and pulled her deeper into his groin. His other hand strayed under her top and cupped her breast.

"This what you want?" he breathed huskily.

She rubbed against him, eager for his hands, his mouth, his throbbing dick-- everything at once. "More." She floated on a cloud of sensual pleasure where everything was deliciously bright, surreal, and control was out of her hands.

His fingers tweaked her nipples, and his mouth found hers. He gave her scorching hot kisses, and she moaned, tossing her head from side to side. His hands moved lower, and she pressed against him.

"Oh, my Gawd, oh, my Gawd. Yes, yes, yes."

His movements became jerky, his hips thrusting, pushing himself deeper into her. She squirmed, trying to get closer as the momentum built. Need, want, lust, made her blood hot. Her sweet spot pushed against his bulge, and he shuddered, touching her where she needed to be touched. She arched her back, and he thrust hard, then let out a bellow, and just like that she came.

With her release, reality came crashing down on her. What had they done?

Chase lifted them out of the chair, carrying her to the bed. He lay down with her and stroked her hair, kissing her softly.

She was too ashamed to respond. She'd totally instigated this entire mess, because her hormones had gone wild with lust. Oh, damn love bug! How could she have allowed this to happen?

"Mila? Are you okay?"

"Yes. No." She shook her head from side to side. "Give me a simpler question."

"You came on to me pretty strong…" He leaned down and kissed her and she immediately sat up, pushing him away. "I should have stopped it, but I didn't."

"My fault. I'm sorry." She ran a hand through her tangled hair, and breathed deeply, trying to calm down. She needed to get out fast, away from him, away from this gorgeous man who could turn her world inside out. "I've got to call AAA."

"We tried doing that, then you had a better idea." He reached out and touched her arm. "Are you sorry?"

"Yes! It was a mistake. Huge mistake." She licked her lips and sucked in another breath. "I don't know what happened. A moment of insanity. You smelled so good, and kiss like a champion, and I..." She felt a headache coming on, and rubbed a spot between her brows.

He laughed, then seeing she was serious, the smile faded. "I know what you felt. This unreal desire, need so strong you want to strip down and get naked. I wanted that too." He stroked her face. "At least we kept our clothes on."

"But you tried to make me leave, and I refused to go. I darn near raped you, didn't I?"

"No, silly woman. I wanted you as much as you wanted me. Still, I'm glad we stopped when we did. We've both got to fight this thing together. Whatever this is, it's bigger than we are."

"Yes, you're right." She touched his face. "I'm sorry."

He put a hand on her shoulder and gave it a friendly squeeze. "Don't be. It's okay. We came to our senses before we went too far."

"Lucky us." Was it too terrible of her to wish they hadn't? "We have to get rid of this love bug." She crossed the room, as far away from him as she could get.

He glanced at her, a worried frown on his handsome face. "Agreed. How?"

"That's the million dollar question, isn't it?"

CUPID

I rode up the mountain with Mila, wanting to make sure she ran into Chase at the Fairmont—and I must admit, I orchestrated all that beautifully, didn't I? Excuse me while I preen, but you have to admit that having the car battery die had been a stroke of genius.

In my expert opinion, I consider tonight a win-win. This little dilemma brought them closer together, not only physically but emotionally. He was genuinely concerned about her, and his fond feelings will grow into something immeasurably deeper and more beautiful than either have known before.

As often as I see couples falling in love, it still bewilders me as to why they fight it so darn hard. Here is Mila, a lovely girl, but all alone and yet she's surrounded by rapturous couples every day in her line of business. Surely, she must want to experience that kind of joyous emotion herself? How could she not?

And Chase — well, he's quite young and has some learning to do. He's more interested in spreading his seed and furthering his career, then settling down with a wife and family of his own. I know that this news reporter job is not where he wants to be—he has grandiose dreams of becoming a celebrated foreign correspondent, but there are only so many of those jobs, aren't they? Dangerous too. Being in a war torn village, or city filled with rebels, and bombs, and bloodshed and mayhem. But this may never come to pass. Or it will, and they will have to sort it out. That will be their decision to make.

My job ends when the two of them fall so deeply in love that they can never find their way out. What they do after that is entirely up to them.

CHAPTER SEVEN

Mila ground her teeth together. "We can't escape. No one has ever gotten rid of it, as far as I know. Look, the best thing we can do is just agree never to see each other again."

She stood up, straightened her clothes, and grabbed her leather jacket. "I'll wait for AAA down in the lobby. I'm sorry." She blinked rapidly, close to tears.

"I'll go with you. It's late, and not safe for you to wait alone." Chase grabbed his key from the counter and shoved it in his jeans pocket.

"No. It's you that I need to get away from! No one's going to bother me in the hotel lobby."

"I suppose you're right, but it could be a long wait." A smile tugged the corner of his mouth. "You had something else on your mind. Something more interesting than jump-starting your car."

"Pulleze—don't remind me!" She cringed and made a face. "You must have found my behavior very strange. To say the least."

"Yeah, you could say that. Although it was more confusing than strange. Still I've got to admit, I'm starting to like this love bug." He grinned, and Mila couldn't help but think how cute he looked with his dimples flashing and the warm glint in his eyes.

If she wasn't so adamantly opposed to falling in love, she could really like him.

"No, you don't. I'm sure you have big plans for your future and they sure in hell don't include me."

"That's true. I don't necessarily mean the not including you part, but I have bigger goals than reporting fluff for WUX News. I intend to be a foreign correspondent one day."

"Really? Why would you want that? Death and bloodshed all around you. Sounds awful."

"My father was a correspondent. He was killed ten years ago. I know I'll never be as good as him, but I want to try."

"I'm sorry about your dad, and for what I said. That was thoughtless of me." She touched his arm. "You must be very proud of him."

"I am. Being a foreign correspondent is all I've ever wanted to be, but I have awfully big shoes to fill." He rubbed his jaw. "I've been with WUX for eight years, and I'm still no closer to getting a job overseas than I was when I first started. Figured that my time would have come by now." He shook his head, with a look of disgust. "With all the wars and uprisings, why am I still sitting here looking for a love bug? I should be out reporting from halfway around the world. Like that's ever going to happen."

"It could." She leaned against the door, and looked at him, trying to understand why he was giving up on his dream. But then she had, hadn't she? "Why not?"

"It's about as likely as winning the lotto. I mean how many journalists can you name? There's maybe a handful that people recognize besides the anchors on the nightly news."

"So how does one go from being a local news reporter to being a foreign correspondent?"

"Like everything in life, it comes down to experience, hard work, being exceptional at what you do at the right time and the right place." He gave a hint of a smile, adding, "Then we factor in luck and who you know. Probably the last two elements are the ones that will get you noticed."

"So your father must have been well known. Doesn't that count for something?"

"I didn't want to use his connections. Figured I could do it on my own, and that isn't working out so well."

"Maybe you need to move. Go to London or something."

"My mother isn't in very good health. She has the beginning of Alzheimer's but still lives alone." He shrugged. "I hired a woman to come in each day. It's the best I can do for now."

"Are you sure that's not just an excuse?" She regretted her question as soon as it was asked. She had been the one to quit, give up on her dreams after her big disappointment. Chase was stronger than that. He couldn't leave his sick mother. It was totally different.

He looked at her like she was crazy. "My brother was killed in Iraq and now I'm all she's got. Soon she won't remember and then I'll be free to leave. I've been training for an overseas post for several years. Studied politics and international relationships in college. Also did some volunteer work for Habitat a couple of summers, over in Poland and Bosnia."

Damn it. Why did he have to be so freaking great? "So, you've basically done everything right. Now, it's just timing and not quitting."

"I guess, but I'm getting restless waiting for the luck part to kick in."

She nodded, keeping up her tough-guy persona. "Well, Chase, I suggest you get your ass out of Serendipity Falls sooner rather than later. Tell your boss that you've seen what happens first hand."

He winked at her. "I've experienced it too."

Swallowing a rush of heat brought on by his charm, she cleared her throat. "So write your story and get out while the getting is good."

"Wish it were that simple. I mean, what do I really have to write about? You and I both got a little feverish and wanted to have sex. So big deal. Most single men and women who are attracted to each other feel similar symptoms."

He was saying exactly what she wanted to hear, which perversely made her argue the counter point. "We know it was different—don't we? I mean, I've never acted like I did tonight. I let go of any inhibition and trust me, that doesn't happen. I don't even sleep around—much."

"Much? Like how much?" he asked, using his reporter's voice.

"Like practically never, and I've never wanted anything as much as I did this."

"This—you mean having sex with me?"

"Yeah, that's what I meant all right." She lifted her chin, and tried to hold back a rush of feelings. He could make her weak, but she needed to be strong.

He patted the bed. "If you change your mind about leaving, we could do something about that."

She stood next to the doorframe, refusing to take those five steps across the room. "True, but that can't happen. Being together is totally stupid. We're playing with fire. And staying here is dangerous to you and your mental health. Your dreams will never come true." She bit her bottom lip, wanting him to understand how important it was to keep going. "I gave mine up years ago, and I don't want to see you do the same."

"You want to tell me about it?"

"No." She straightened her shoulders and looked him in the eye. "I certainly do not. I have regrets, but on the other hand I love my shop and I'm making good money at it. Enough that I can always pursue my other hobby later in life."

"What kind of hobby?"

Couldn't take the reporter out of the man, it seemed. "If I tell you that, then I have to tell you what my dreams were."

"So tell me," he said, his open expression inviting her to spill her guts. "It's not like I'm going to write about it.

I want to know what makes you tick. Why are you so driven in your business, and anti-dating?"

She never shared her past as a matter of principle. But if it made him realize that he needed to get out of Serendipity in pursuit of what really mattered, then maybe it was important. She sighed. "I was a show jumper. It was my passion." Bittersweet memories flooded her. There had been glory days, basking in the sunshine with her horse, hearing the applause of the crowd as she won blue ribbons. Happiness, youthful joy, and first love that crashed down around her, driving her dreams into the muck.

"I wanted to pursue a career as an equestrian, either riding, showing, or training. Anything that involved my love of horses."

He studied her. "So why did you give it up?"

She wouldn't give him the emotional details. "Private reasons. I stopped riding." She snapped her fingers. "Like that. Walked away from what could have been an amazing career."

"Wow. Must have been something big," he said thoughtfully. "A man?"

"Now why would you think that?" She didn't even flinch. "I was talking horses, not men."

"Had to be something that shook your world, or you'd have kept doing what you loved."

She didn't say anything. It didn't matter anymore. Nothing mattered except to keep on doing what she was doing. Enjoying family and friends, working hard, stashing money away for a rainy day.

He rubbed his jaw. "Maybe after a few more years working the boutique, you could buy your own stable of horses."

His words echoed her thoughts. She turned around, her hand at the door. "Maybe. We'll see." She gave him a brief smile. "I've got to go."

He moved quickly and was by her side. "I wish you'd stay."

"I know." Funny thing was, she knew he meant it. Conversation, getting to know one another. Even without sex. "I can't."

"Are you sure you'll be all right?"

"Yes." She kept her head lowered, wanting to get away from him fast. Before she made a huge mistake. Before they both did.

He placed his hands on both her shoulders and turned her around. "Mila. Look at me." He hooked a finger under her jaw and lifted up her face. "Don't give up on your dreams."

"Same back at you. You need to go to dangerous war zones and give your insightful reports."

"Or we could stay right here and fall in love." He pulled her slowly toward him and gently kissed her mouth.

She returned the kiss and instant heat flared. She felt sizzled from her tiptoes all the way to the roots of her hair. Her tummy flopped around like a baby seal, and her pulse fluttered like butterfly wings.

Her poor customers. So, this is what it felt like. Insane. Insatiable. Incomprehensible.

"I must go." She pushed away. "I've got to go."

"Or you could stay."

"Goodbye, Chase. Best of luck with getting what you want." She turned and hurried out.

* * *

Chase ran a hand over his head, wondering what he could have done to change her mind. He knew she was probably saving them both from a lifetime of hell, but he sure could have used a good night or two wrapped in her arms, releasing some of this friction between them.

He'd always been a bit of a ladies man, not by choice exactly, but girls seemed to dig his dimples and he had his old man to thank for that. That was the one thing his father gave him before taking off. The story he'd fed Mila? Hadn't happened, but it was certainly better than the truth.

He hadn't heard hide or hair from his father in the past two decades. How could a man ditch his wife and forget his sons for all of twenty years? Well, the son-of-a-bitch might be dead for all he knew. He sure in hell had never helped his mother any. No one had.

His mother had ended up marrying some loser who used to beat the crap out of her. Lucky for her, the jerk had been tossed in jail on some drug charge. His mom got factory work but the long hours standing at a conveyor belt had given her chronic back pain. The dreary job had stolen her health, her beauty and youth. She was only fifty, but she looked broken and old. Like he'd told Mila—she had early signs of Alzheimer's and Chase needed to take care of her as he'd tried in the past.

Chase and his brother, Josh, had done their share growing up to lighten her load. They both had paper routes and mowed lawns, shoveled snow, whatever they could to help pay the bills and put food on the table. His brother had ended up quitting school and worked in the factory too. He hadn't gone off to Iraq and died a hero. That was just another story he liked to tell. Sounded a lot better then saying his brother had gotten drunk, jumped on his motorcycle and collided with a post. After his high school graduation Chase didn't stick around.

He'd worked his ass off to get a partial scholarship and had put himself through college, all the while working twenty hours a week as a valet at a ritzy club. The ladies had tipped him good. They'd also given him tokens of their appreciation when he'd drive them home at night.

By his junior year he had enough money that he didn't park cars or service women, and it allowed him to further his ambitions. He spent two summers building for Habitat and learning Italian and German, a leg up for his career.

Why would he jeopardize all that just for the love of a woman? He'd had plenty of female company in the past, but nothing had ever purged the emptiness inside of him or the hunger to make something of his life.

CHAPTER EIGHT

It took Mila a couple of hours to get her car up and running and return home, and she had lots of time to mentally kick herself black and blue. She should never have gone to the Fairmont, or to Mammoth, or anywhere in the vicinity of that man, knowing all that she knew about the crazy shit that went on around here.

She knew it couldn't be controlled or remedied because plenty of people had tried. Her brother for one. He'd gone into a health food store looking for some kind of antidote. No way had he wanted to get married and settle down—he had a few financial concerns and was barely scratching out a living. Devon and Kyle were co-owners of the Cock and Bull bar, which made megabucks in the winter months, and zip in the summer.

But for all his wanting, his ranting and his considerable will, he'd been unable to break the curse and had been carried along on the road of love, ergo fighting and screaming every inch of the way.

Stronger men than her had tried and failed. The only possible way to dodge this bullet would be to never, ever see Chase again. But that thought made her sad. He was a sweet guy and he needed to get his story and high-tail it out of here before some other female walked by and his feelings for Mila might transfer to her.

Damn, it was all a mess. She didn't want him getting snagged by some awful man-eater, one of the hungry cougars on the prowl looking for young, fresh blood. She had seen them coming in by the busloads, hanging around the bars, buying clothes too tight, too short, and too young, from the shops in the mall. They would parade around in their skimpy clothes, peroxide hair and fake boobs, hoping to catch themselves a husband.

Poor Chase. That would suck big time. A woman like that wouldn't fit into his plans as a foreign correspondent—matter-of-fact, in certain countries that might get her stoned, not by good grass either.

What could she do to help him, without ending up toast?

She climbed into bed that night, and tossed and turned wondering what would have happened had she not come to her senses when she did. He'd been eager to get inside her pants and she'd wanted him there too. Had they actually made love, well, it might have made the connection between them harder to break. She'd been nineteen the last time she'd had an orgasm due to heavy petting. Having sex with Chase? She'd combust. That would make her weak and clingy, and she so wasn't going there.

"That's it," she told herself. The solution to their immediate problem. She could help with his story, wave him goodbye, and as long as they didn't consummate their union they might be safe.

It all sounded so plausible as the sun peaked through her window blinds. No harm done. They were still two separate people with a will of their own. As long as they didn't physically unite, there'd be no bond. They could be free of each other and go their own ways. It made perfect sense. No sex, no bond, no love, or wedding, or happily forever after.

Oh, thank heavens! She could remain alone for the rest of her days.

The next time she ran into him--and she was pretty sure she would, doubting that he'd heed her warning and stay clear, well, she'd tell him she had a workable plan. As long as they didn't sleep together, they'd be safe.

What would he think if she told him she thought Serendipity Falls had its own angel? Not a bug at all. It might change the direction of his story.

* * *

The following day, her brother Kyle came into town and invited her to lunch. Since she hadn't seen him in weeks, she agreed and closed her shop for an hour, putting a sign on the door to let her customers know she'd be back at one.

They met at the restaurant overlooking the falls. The food was better than at the mall as they had home baked bread, freshly made soups and always a couple of specials of the day.

Sue Burke handed them their menus and asked if they'd like some water. Both declined.

"So what's up?" she asked Kyle, who was two years older than herself. He had a girlfriend who was a ski instructor, but had somehow avoided the marriage trap. She'd like to know how.

"Nothing much. I had to come here for some supplies. Picked up a load of stuff at Costco, enough paper products and household items to last us all summer." He leaned back in the booth, and ran a hand through his mop of curls. His hair was always long and unruly, but it suited him, just as the mountain life did.

"Well, I'm glad you called. Haven't seen you in a while, and I've been wondering how you're making out. Now that Devon's moving in with Tara, are you going to invite Lisa to move in?"

"I might. I know she's been hinting at that. I like her a lot, but I'm just not ready for that kind of commitment, you know?"

"Are you ever going to be? You've been dating for nearly two years, it's no wonder she wants a little more from you." She tilted her head back to look at him. "You still look like a kid, but you're thirty-one. How did you manage to stay single living in this place?"

"It's not easy, but I never drink the water. Not from a tap, not bottled either."

"You think that's the trick?" She looked up as Sue approached. "I'll have a diet coke and your soup and sandwich special."

"Me too," Kyle said. "Make mine the onion soup and the corned beef on rye."

"Lentil for me, and a BLT. Thanks, Sue." Mila fiddled with the salt and pepper shakers. "So, do you love Lisa?"

"Sure. Kind of. Just not ready for that whole marriage thing. She wants kids, and I do—eventually. Not ready yet."

"I get it. I really like Lisa, and would love to have some nieces or nephews to spoil, but I'm not in any hurry to marry or have kids either. My wedding business has my complete attention."

"I know you're doing great with your boutique but whatever happened with your riding? You were horse crazy, then you just gave it up. I always thought that was odd, the way you sold Lady so quickly."

"I grew out of it, I suppose. It was a teenage thing and I knew I had to go to college and find a real career."

"You were good, and I thought you'd always keep up the jumping, even if it was just a hobby."

"An expensive hobby. And when Gram and Pops died, well, keeping Lady and riding brought up a lot of painful memories."

"Hmm. Funny. I always wondered if it had something to do with that guy you were seeing. Wasn't he married?"

"He was, but I don't want to talk about him. I want to know how to avoid whatever the heck is going on around here. We have reporters asking questions, people buying up property and moving in. This is not just our little myth anymore—the town is becoming famous. And I'm afraid."

"Of what? You've proven to be quite resourceful. Dodging the love bug but profiting highly from it. This is a win-win for your shop and for Mammoth too. Matter of fact, this summer Dev and I are expecting to make a good profit. Pay our bank loan off."

"That's great news. I'm really happy for you, and I know it's good for Serendipity and the ski village, but I don't like all the strangers crawling around. I liked having the town to ourselves. Just us locals."

"It's called growth, sis. We're going to have schools built, a bigger hospital, better roads. More commerce, more people, and more recreation. It'll be a great place to live. To eventually raise a family."

"It already is. Always has been." She waited until Sue dropped off their sodas and soups before speaking again. She kept her eyes lowered and whispered, "I've been infected."

He'd picked up his soup spoon and now it fell out of his hand, clattering on the wooden table. "You don't mean…"

"I do." She sipped her soda, her eyes on his. "I'm scared, Kyle."

"Tell me." Kyle looked behind her as the front door opened and two men walked in. "Wait a sec. The reporters just walked in. They came into the bar yesterday, asking a bunch of questions. Have you met them yet?"

Her knees began to shake, and every inch of her grew hot. She felt feverish, her skin on fire, but as cold as ice underneath. She didn't need to turn her head to know that Chase was standing there. The flames in her body leapt out, almost as though seeking a refuge.

"Mila." Chase stood next to their table, and his face looked as red hot as hers felt. He had this fever thing too.

Kyle looked from one to the other. "Shit. No."

"Get away from me," she squeaked, and noticed Mike took a seat at the counter. "Go sit with him," she pointed.

"Forget Mike. What are you doing here?" Chase asked. "Why aren't you at the shop?" He glanced at Kyle and his eyes narrowed. "Who are you?"

"I'm her brother and you better back off, buddy. She doesn't look too well, and whatever you've done to her better stop." Kyle put a protective hand over hers, and then quickly snatched it away. "Holy crap. You're burning hot."

Mila's eyes filled and refreshing tears spilled down her cheeks. "We're both infected," she told Kyle. "It's not his fault. Or mine, but we have to figure out a way to get rid of it. What can we do?"

Kyle jumped up, and stepped away from the booth. "Hell if I know. I love you, sis, but I've got to get out of here in case it's contagious." He grabbed his jacket and shrugged into it. "You'll figure something out."

"You coward," she cried. "How can you leave me like this?"

"Sorry to say but you're on your own." He backed up, his eyes going from Mila to Chase. "He looks like a decent guy. You could do worse."

"Don't you dare leave me!" She shot him looks to kill. "I'll tell Devon and Tara. Even Lisa. You…you…" she sputtered, "you wimp. You flake!"

Sue came forward. "I'm here, honey. What can I get you? Need some iced water? Your face is awfully flushed."

"No! No! Definitely not water. Jeez, why is this happening to me?"

Kyle tossed some money down and ran for the door. "Good luck. I'll see you at the wedding."

"Hope you get bitten, you chicken shit," she called after him.

Mike sat alone at the counter, smiling and shaking his head. Chase ignored his friend and slipped into the seat that Kyle had just vacated. "Might as well eat. No sense letting this go to waste." He picked up the spoon and dipped it into the piping hot soup. "Who's wedding was he talking about?" he asked, waiting for the spoonful to cool. "Ours?"

She closed her eyes and banged her head against the back of the hard, wooden booth a few times. Then she sucked in a painful breath. Finally when she was calm, she opened her eyes and hissed, "We are not getting married. Not now. Not ever. Get that into your head."

"Okay. Fine with me. Now eat. We'll talk about it later."

"There is no later. There is nothing to discuss. You and I, we're through. Whatever that means since we never even started." She laughed, feeling hysteria bubbling inside. "Consider this --I'm breaking up with you. Forever."

She picked up her soda, stood up and dumped it over his head. "Maybe that will cool you down." Before he could say a word, she was halfway to the door. "Matter-of-fact you can put that in your story."

CHAPTER NINE

Sue came over with a wet towel and clucked over him as he mopped up. "I'm so sorry. I've never seen her act this way. Normally, she's a lovely girl. You must have done something to get her so riled up."

"Wasn't me," he answered, not liking the accusation in her voice. "Whatever's going on in this town is the problem between us. You know anything about it?"

"Oh my!" Her eyes grew big and her cheeks rosy. "You mean you are victims of the love bug? Oh, how perfectly romantic. You are so lucky. Count your blessings, young man. She really is a very sweet girl. Doing very well with that shop of hers too." She glanced over at his friend. "You fellows from a newspaper or TV?"

Chase mumbled, "TV." He kept his head down, eyeing the onion soup.

"Well, just think! What an interesting story this will turn out to be!" She raised her voice and told the other customers, "This man here is a reporter, and he's got the bug. Isn't that wonderful?"

His head shot up. "Lady, this is the worst thing that can happen. I don't want to end up in this hick town. I've got places to go. Important things to do."

"Well, no more, my friend. Now the most important thing in your life will be making babies." She laughed, and shoved Kyle's money on him. "This lunch is on me, you might need that extra cash."

Chase stood up and walked over to Mike, who was wearing a Texas sized grin. "Well, I guess the cat's out of the bag. You might as well go home, but I've got to stay here. Tell the boss that I'm taking a leave of absence, but when I get back he'll have his story. In full."

"You don't want to do this man," Mike said in earnest now. "Come back with me. You get away from here, you might be all right. Save yourself. Don't sacrifice your entire life for this miserable story."

Chase's shoulders dropped.

Mike stood up and took Chase by the elbow. "Forget this. We'll go home."

Chase shook off his hand. "No. As much as I'd like to hightail it out of here, I have to stay and figure this out. If I know what it is, then I'll know how to get rid of it, right?"

"Maybe, maybe not," Mike said and stepped away. "Wonder if it's catchy."

"No idea, but you better clear out. Don't worry about me." He grinned, but it was an effort. "I'm not letting this get the best of me. No friggin' way. You'll see. Might even win the Pulitzer Prize in journalism too."

"Dream on, bro. This isn't that big a deal," Mike said. "To you it may be, but not to the rest of the world." He gave him a long look. "You really don't look well. Your pupils are dilated and you're all hot and sweaty. Worse, you're not thinking clearly. Best thing you can do is leave here now and never come back."

"I'm not leaving. Not until I know what the hell is going on." Chase glanced around at the few customers who were listening to their every word. "Does anybody here know what's causing this wedding fever? Is it something environmental? Maybe something that happened when the place was being mined?" When no one spoke up, he added, "If it's an environmental issue, we can get the place cleaned up. The government will owe you big time. Make you all rich."

One guy spoke up. "What? And stop the weddings? We like things the way they are around here."

"You guys are happy with this situation? You're all sitting ducks. Could happen to you at any minute. What's wrong with you people? Doesn't anybody believe in free will?"

The few men sitting in booths shook their heads and went back to their food. If anyone knew anything, it was obvious they weren't talking. Not to a reporter, that's for damn sure.

"You think that's what it is?" Mike whispered. "Some biological waste or mineral that drifted into their water stream?"

"Heck if I know. Your guess is as good as mine."

"Okay. You find out what it is. It'll make a hell of a story, man." Mike clapped him on the shoulder. "Take care of yourself. And stay away from that woman."

Chase nodded and went to the bathroom to wash up. After giving Mike enough time to leave, he took off like lightning had hit him, determined to have a word with Mila before she went back to work. He ran into the parking lot and saw her Range Rover. He glanced across the street, and started walking toward the falls. Something told him she'd be there.

He found her sitting on a log, her head thrown back, watching the giant waterfall as it gushed and flowed down the mountain side, pooling in the emerald lake below. It was a breath-taking sight, but no more so than the beautiful young woman who sat there looking dazed and defeated.

The crunch of the broken leaves and underbrush gave his footsteps away, but she didn't turn her head. It was as though she expected him.

He sat down next to her. Picked up her hand and put it in his lap. "What are we going to do? We can't surrender to this. We have to fight it somehow."

"I don't know how." She left her hand where it was but still didn't look at him.

He sat in silence for some time, listening to the song birds, the roar of the rushing water, the sounds of creatures scurrying around in the bush, her soft sighs. He knew she was trying to come to terms with the unacceptable, and he wished her luck with that, because he had the same dilemma as well.

"We could just ignore it and maybe it would go away," he suggested.

"That won't work. I'm sure others have tried."

"Has anyone ever broken the spell?"

"Not that I know of." She darted a look his way. "Why didn't you just leave? I was sitting here hoping and praying that you would drive away and never come back."

"No, you weren't. You knew I would find you here." He raised her hand and kissed it. "You were waiting for me."

"Why do you say that?" Her voice was monotone, without expression. Her vibrant personality was held captive too. He wanted to free them both so they could go back to their real lives, to the people they were before.

"Because you weren't surprised to see me," he told her quietly. "You weren't afraid of who might be creeping up on you. You knew all along it was me."

"So what does that prove?" Her voice was listless, her face slack, as if every powerful emotion inside of her had bled out.

He felt like smashing something. This wooden doll was not the fiery Mila O'Reilley he knew her to be.

"It proves that you're not afraid of me, and yet I'm the very person you should most fear." He slipped an arm around her shoulders and gave her a little shake, hoping to dislodge her lethargy. "You okay?"

"Guess so. But I don't have anything to fear from you." She glanced up at him, seeming to wake up a little. "We're in this together, and we have to fight it together."

"I'm glad you agree, because I sent Mike home, and I'm staying until I can figure this thing out. Once I know what it is, I, or we, will have a chance to overcome it."

"No one knows. Everyone has some idea, but no one knows anything for sure. I don't believe it's a love bug.

Never heard of such a thing, not even in folklore. I've googled it and came up with nothing."

"So what is your hunch then?"

She swallowed hard. Then laughed and turned watery eyes up to meet his. "It's just as crazy. Maybe crazier." She licked her lips. "Okay. Are you ready for this? I have two theories, both equally ridiculous. One, I think it might be Venus, the goddess of Love. Maybe she's been assigned Serendipity Falls, and we are under her benevolent grace. Hell if I know." When he didn't laugh, she went on. "The other idea is that it could be an angel. Occasionally I've heard the sound of wings fluttering nearby."

Overhead, they heard a small branch of a tree as it snapped and broke. They watched it fall out of the sky and land a mere few feet from where the two of them sat.

"That was close," she murmured.

"You're safe with me." He smiled. "So back to your theories. I don't know if they are ridiculous or not, but both are incredibly romantic. Didn't know you had it in you."

"I don't. I'm a clear headed business woman, with a heap of trouble on my hands." She bumped shoulders with him. "Namely you."

He bumped back. "I prefer to think that it has a more logical explanation. Perhaps something from the gold mining days. Maybe a certain mineral in the spring water, or pollution in the air. Environmental, that's what I think."

"Well, that might be easier to prove than an angel or Venus, so I hope you're right."

"So do I." He held out his hand. "You want to head back? I need a ride into town. Mike took the truck. I'm on my own."

"You got a place to stay?"

"The hotel up in Mammoth. I'm still officially working this story." He looked at her with caution. "You know a better place?"

"If you stay with me maybe we can figure this out sooner. But on one condition—that you promise no matter how much I want you and tempt you, that you will under no circumstance make love to me."

"What do you take me for? A eunuch?"

She laughed. "No. A gentleman. Can we do this or not?"

"We can certainly try. If nothing else, it'll be interesting and I'll get some first-hand knowledge for my story."

"Yes. That you will." She linked arms with him. "Hopefully it'll only be a matter of days. You can use my car when I'm working and go dig around. Maybe some of the old timers will know something we don't."

"Speaking of work, aren't you late opening today?"

"I opened up at ten, and took a couple of hours off. So sue me. My customers don't like it, they can go to another wedding planner/bridal shop in town."

"I thought you owned the only one."

"You got that right, so what choice do they have?"

"About as much as we do right now. But I'll drop you off at the mall then chase around town and see what I can find. What time should I pick you up?"

"Six?" she asked, with a hint of a smile.

"Six it is. And I'll take you for dinner." When they got to her car, he opened the passenger door and helped her in. Not that he needed to, but it did give him a nice view of her sweet tush. "What time did the tow truck get to you last night?"

"Wasn't bad. I had to wait about an hour. I was home a little after midnight."

"You're going to be tired tonight." He jumped into the driver's seat, and she handed him the keys. "You got two beds?"

"No, but you can sleep on the sofa." She glanced straight ahead. "I sure hope we know what we're doing."

"We're going to solve this problem, put it behind us, and get on with our lives. That's what we're doing."

"Okay." She swallowed. "I'm putting my trust in you." Her hazelnut eyes met his then slid away. "Don't let me down."

"I won't. I want out of here as much as you want me to go."

She licked her bottom lip and he saw it tremble. He very much wanted to kiss her soft mouth and hold her tight--tight enough to make her feel safe and to erase both their fears.

Instead he started the car, put it in gear and gunned it. The last thing he wanted, he needed, was another moment in her company. She evoked all the emotions he fought to control, and stroked a fire that called for extinction.

Living with her even for a few days, surrounded by her sight, her scent, her physical closeness, and knowing how much they wanted to sleep together—hell, it would be pure torture, but they both had to remind themselves it was a means to an end.

CUPID

An angel? Oh, my goodness, but that got me hopping mad. Yes, even charming, gentle, loving Cupids can get mad. We shouldn't, of course, but it does happen from time to time and I'm embarrassed to say that I let my emotions get the better of me.

I'd been sitting in a tree watching and listening as Mila confided in Chase, and at the mention of an angel I'd become so incensed that I jumped up and down, nearly falling out of the tree. The branch had cracked, and darn near landed on the bewildered couple's heads. Would have served them right too!

She admitted hearing the fluttering of wings but not once did she think of me. It breaks my heart, it really does. No one ever thinks of me unless it's Valentine's Day. Then they buy all those delicious chocolates with hearts and flowers, and cute little cards with pictures of Cupid and his crafty arrow. Suddenly, I'm everywhere. But for the rest of the year I'm vanished, out of sight and out of mind—like I don't exist at all. Oh, it does bruise my heart.

I want to be loved, like everyone else. Held in high esteem. Yes, I do, and it's my failing. My pride is my weakness, and for that I'm ashamed.

But little Mila must learn the error of her ways. She won't like what I'm about to plan for her next, but she certainly has it coming.

Tee-hee, tee-hee. It's all so much fun and not mean spirited at all. Although she may not know it now, the sweet surrender will bring her lasting happiness. As for the young buck, well, he might not be thrilled about never seeing first-hand action in war torn countries, but with my helping hand he might win a coveted prize for literature. And be somewhere safe and loved.

Surely, that's worth more in the long run. It's not like I don't take into account the dreams and ambitions of the people I zap with my bow and arrow. The point is I actually believe that I know them better than they know themselves. Besides, I'm a romantic, through and through.

Take today for example. Here I was sitting in the tree, enjoying myself quite immensely at first. I was able to gaze out and see the beginning of new life everywhere I glanced. Love was all around me. Two sparrows sat in a tree across and I could feel their connection. Butterflies were mating, flowers were blooming, busy bees spread pollen, fresh grass was budding, and the warmth of spring graced the air.

Happiness bubbled inside of me until I heard the whispered words out of Mila's sweet mouth. Venus! An angel? Oh, dear beloved ones, what about me?

CHAPTER TEN

After Chase dropped Mila at the mall, he went back to the hotel, checked out, and then walked around the village interviewing people, asking old timers about the long ago mining days. He also drove to the nearest municipal building and requested any pertinent documents regarding the still active mines, and googled the area extensively, digging for anything that might mention any hazardous waste or environmental issues.

He came up short.

Not entirely empty handed, he picked up Mila bearing a couple of bottles of wine and two good steaks.

"Did you find anything out?" she asked hopefully. Seeing his expression, her smile faded. "Chase. What if you can't find out what this is? How long will you stay?"

"Just a few days either way. I don't want to leave until I know, but staying will make things worse. Besides, I can always report about the effects, firsthand. Might make for some interesting TV." He rubbed a hand over his jaw. "It'll give my female readers some titillation, I'm sure."

She gave a hollow laugh. "You could write a book. Make it hot. Turn it into a best seller."

"It's hot all right. That's the problem." His eyes lingered on her face, and settled on her sexy mouth. "Just looking at you makes me want to do you every which way but Sunday."

"Oh, crap." She bit her bottom lip. "Then don't look at me."

"That might be hard." He started walking. "How about if you follow me?"

She raced up beside him. "I'm not going to walk two paces behind you like some unliberated woman from years gone by. No way in hell."

"Whatever. Just go with the flow then. I'm not going to act on my feelings, I just want you to know that I have them."

"Roger that and ditto back." She kept walking, keeping her head down, so he couldn't see into her face.

Her neck seemed a little flushed though. "All right. I think it's good that we don't keep anything secret between us. It's important that we're upfront with our emotions so neither of us gets confused."

"I agree. Also, talking about it will make it easier to manage."

He kept his eyes straight ahead, although it was difficult walking a straight line with the swelling between his legs. Felt like he had a hammer jammed into his pants. "Why do women like to talk about their emotions all the time and men prefer to just act on them?"

She glanced at him. "You're primal beasts." She laughed. "Women aren't afraid to have feelings, but you guys seem to think its unmanly or something."

"No, we have them, but don't romanticize it. If we see a woman we like we want to have sex with her. That's all."

"That's all?" She shot him an angry glance. "You just want to get your rocks off?"

"I didn't say that. It's just simpler for us. More physical, less emotional, at least until we fall in love."

"I see." Her voice turned frosty. "Well, we will make damn sure that doesn't happen."

"Oh, don't get testy. You know we both don't want it, so let's keep it that way. We're in this together." He held the door as she brushed past him to exit the mall.

"Where's the car?" she snapped.

"Follow me and you'll find out." He took off and she had to run to keep up. He turned around, jogging backward, goading her for no reason except that he was enjoying it. Preferable to hanging around her dangling a hard-on, that's for sure.

He stopped when he reached the car and sat on the back fender to watch her. "Hey slow poke, can't you keep up?" he teased when she drew near.

She was breathing hard and didn't look amused. "Give me the keys," she demanded.

"Find them," he answered, lifting his arms in the air.

"Give. Me. The. Keys." She took two steps toward him, and held out her hand.

He laughed and took them out of his pocket. "Come and get them." He stood tall and raised them above his head.

She lunged for them, and he lifted them higher. She reached again, and the movement carried her forward until they were chest to chest.

He watched the expressions on her face change. Her hazel eyes began to glow, turning from brown to green, cheeks turned rosy, and her mouth opened invitingly.

Oh hell. Oh shit. He'd been playing with fire, and it had flared up and was about to bite him in the ass.

"Here. Take them." He shoved the set of keys in her hand and stepped back, feeling the hair raise on the back of his neck. It was like the last time—back in his hotel room when she'd come prancing out of the bathroom.

She'd been the predator and he the prey.

"Where are you going?" she asked, stepping toward him. "You want to play, don't you?" She tilted her nose up in the air while her cat's eyes danced merrily. "Let's play."

"My mistake." He put his arms out to keep her at a distance. "Back off. Get away from me."

She laughed. "You really are a chicken shit." She unlocked the doors then jumped into the driver seat, and leaned over to open his door. "You coming?"

"Am I safe?" He glanced at her, annoyed at how the tables had turned. He'd been fooling around. He wasn't at all sure about her.

"You'll have to enter to find out."

"Look, I've got my belongings in your car, but maybe it would be best if I find a hotel."

"Cluck, cluck, cluck." She shrugged her shoulders. "Suit yourself, little chickie."

"You really know how to piss a guy off." Cautiously he eased himself into the passenger seat, keeping one hand on the door.

"Oh, give it a rest. I'm just messing with you."

He wanted to believe that, but he could see the heat rising from her collar and the way she licked her lips. He'd experienced this flipped side of her before, and once bit, twice shy.

"What do you want with me, anyway?"

"Same thing you do. Answers. And there's only one way to find out. Go to the source of the fire." She glanced at him. "You man enough to try?"

"We took an oath that nothing would happen between you and me. Sex is off the table. Right?"

"If you say so."

She licked her lips again. And why the hell did that have to look so damn sexy? He stretched his legs and tried to ease the tightness in his crotch.

"We agreed on that. No sex. Not even close." Changing the subject, he said, "I bought some steaks and some wine. You play backgammon? Maybe we could have a game or two after dinner."

"We can have a game or two," she said in a sultry voice. "But I think I'd prefer strip poker."

Crikey! He was in serious trouble. She was either really enjoying messing with his head, or she intended to have chicken, namely him, as a home cooked meal.

CHAPTER ELEVEN

Mila parked in the small one car garage and entered through the mudroom, turning on lights. Chase was right behind her and nearly tripped over something that hissed at him.

"That's Charlie. Biggest damn cat I ever saw, but he's a great mouse catcher. You think I feed him too much?"

Chase glanced down at the orange tabby cat that looked the size of a Texas linebacker and raised his eyes to hers. "How big are the mice?"

"Well, he does get an occasional rat. Don't you, baby?" She bent down and cuddled the monster cat, then opened a fresh can of tuna and dumped it in his bowl.

"Guess he's good for protection. Nobody would mess with him."

"That's what I figured." Mila felt a little uncomfortable suddenly, having Chase in her place. Now that she had him here, what was she going to do with him? "I'll get the heater on while you bring in your things."

"Any rats in the garage?"

"What? Don't tell me you're scared. You want Charlie to come out with you?"

"I'd be a whole lot happier, but I doubt that he'll leave a full bowl of tuna. I'll just man up and go get my stuff."

She laughed. "Scream if you run into trouble."

He made a face. "You could come with me. For protection."

"I think you can handle it." Smiling, she watched him go. He was a bit of a wuss, but she didn't mind. It would make this tricky situation easier to control.

He brought in two bags of groceries and dumped them on the counter then headed back for his personal belongings. "Where do you want me to stash this stuff?"

She glanced at his duffle bag, his laptop computer, and a beat-up guitar.

"Find a spot someplace. You won't be here that long." She nodded toward the guitar. "Recreation, or looking for a new line of work?"

He grinned. "Hardly. I'm not much good but I like to play. Since we drove up here I was able to bring it along."

"I don't mind a little music once in awhile." She motioned to his laptop. "I'm set up with Wi-Fi and also have a printer and fax. You should be able to work from here."

"Sounds good. Thanks."

She started putting the groceries away and he looked for a place to store his stuff. "You can work off the kitchen table," she said, "and sleep on the couch."

He dropped his things next to the sofa and looked as uncomfortable as she was beginning to feel. They'd be tripping over each other if they weren't careful, but it would only be for a short, limited time.

The one bedroom cabin had a large living area, an open kitchen, and a bathroom. There were two large overstuffed sofas, a large square wooden coffee table sitting on a woven Navaho rug, and for company at night she had a flat screen fifty-inch TV. A good sized wall unit was loaded with books and pictures and trinkets, and a stone fireplace took up another wall.

There was a white fur rug in front of the fire, and a mantle above where she displayed her trophies. Had she known she'd be having company, she'd have packed them up and put them under her bed. Why she kept them around, she didn't know. Perhaps as a reminder of what she'd given up and why she'd allowed herself to get sidetracked from her goals. The sight of them reinforced her belief-- no man was worth that, and no man would deter her again.

He spotted them and wandered over. "What's this?" he asked, picking up one and reading the inscription. "Wellington, June 13th/2006, winner of the Open Division."

"Show Jumping. I competed for about six years when I was young."

He looked at another one. "Kansas. Amateur division." He moved from one to the other. "Looks like you were pretty good."

"Yeah, not bad for a dork."

"I don't see you as the dorky type." He turned to face her with a penetrating look, as though he wanted more than a simple answer. "Why did you give it up?"

"It's an expensive hobby, and then my grandparents died. They bought me the horse. I named her Lucky Lady."

"Where is Lucky Lady now?"

"In Napa, but the owners don't compete anymore. Their daughter jumped for a while, but I think it was more her parent's passion than hers. Once she stopped they turned Lady into a brood mare and she had a foal every year."

"They keep the foals or sell them off?"

"It's a business –they sold them, of course."

"Poor Lucky Lady." He looked at the fire. "Mind if I start a fire? It's not exactly cold in here, but I haven't had a fireplace in years."

"Go right ahead. I'm just going to change clothes and then I'll start dinner."

"Take your time." She watched him light a presto log, then layer the fire with the wood she'd placed in a large copper pot. "You can open some red wine if you like," she told him.

"I'll do that."

Mila took a quick shower then put on a pair of jeans and a Lakers Tee-shirt and flip-flops before returning to face this near stranger she could barely take her eyes off.

If she had to have a major crush on a guy, why couldn't he be dog ugly or have bad breath or incurable hiccups or something? Why did he have to be handsome, intelligent, and nice? She hated nice. Nice was too easy to like and she didn't want to like him. Or any man. Not that way. It was okay to have casual sex once in a while. After all, she wasn't a nun. But she didn't want to *like* the guy, like really, really *like* him.

She quickly ran a brush through her hair, put on a smidgen of lipstick, and braced her shoulders as she walked into the room.

He had two glasses of wine poured and stood next to the fire. He turned and handed her one. The glow of the fire captured the beauty of his face, the perfection of his well-built body, the golden glints in his hair.

Dear God in heaven. Why did he have such dreamy blue eyes and movie-star dimples? That was not playing it fair. Whoever had sent this man into town and shot him up with a love bug or whatever the hell it was, was simply not playing by the rules.

This was a stacked game--playing with a loaded deck.

She took the glass from his hand and held it steady, although her fingers trembled as did her knees. With his back to the fire, his beautiful face was aglow. Blue eyes glittered. Mouth full and sensual. He gazed at her as if she were Aphrodite herself.

She wanted to kick some sense into him, and into her. This was going to be one of the most dangerous, agonizing nights of her life. If they survived this without getting forever burned, well maybe they'd have a fighting chance.

But right now she wouldn't bet on it.

He touched the rim of her glass with his own. "Cheers. To a great story."

"Yes, and to moving on with our lives." She took a sip, her eyes still on his. "We will be the first couple to break this spell. That will make this story of yours something really special." She smiled, knowing what he wanted more than anything. He just needed to be reminded, and often. "Award winning. You will make a name for yourself."

A pulse jumped in his cheek and his eyes flashed. "That's right. We'll find out what's behind this wedding fever and our discovery will make me a regular on the nightly news. Anchorman, even."

"Exactly." She moved away from him, heading for the kitchen, eager to put the counter between them. Keep a safe distance from him at all times would not only be smart but essential to ending this craziness between them.

"Want me to season the steaks, or chop something up for a salad," he asked, stepping into her space.

"No! No," she shooed him away. "Go sit down, watch some TV. I'll get things ready. There's not enough room in the kitchen for both of us." Or in my life, she added silently.

"I want to help. It's the least I can do."

"No, the least you can do is to keep out of my way so I can put dinner together and we can eat. Maybe after we can put our heads together and figure out the mystery of this place." She sighed, and dared a glance in his direction. "What a service we'll be doing. Knowing what the cause is will enable people to avoid it if they choose."

He chuckled. "Sounds good to me. Okay, mind if I turn on the news?"

"No, please, by all means do."

Mila busied herself in the kitchen, sneaking glances at Chase through lowered lashes. He was cute, fun, sexy. The kind of guy she might enjoy having around, if she wasn't so solidly against the idea of letting a man close enough to once again ruin her life.

There was too much chemistry between them to be friends, or even to think about casual sex. When she'd bumped into him trying to get the keys, well, something electric had happened and her entire body had burst into heat. She'd tingled all over and felt a strong pull in her female parts, and this was exactly what she was afraid of. How could she sleep behind that door tonight and not think about him lying on the sofa, sexy, warm, and so damn alluringly close?

Maybe she should ask him to chain her to the bed to prevent her from escaping and doing something they both would enjoy but neither of them wanted. That might be the only way either of them would sleep tonight.

The image of what they could be doing instead flooded her brain, and the wine glass slid from her hands and dropped to the floor. Charlie mewed and dashed away. Chase jumped up and was at her side within seconds.

He grabbed her hands to inspect them. "You cut yourself." She only had a minor slice on her baby finger but he lifted it so sweetly and rinsed it under the tap. "Do you have a band aid?"

"In my bathroom. Not the guest one."

"Move away from the glass and I'll go get it, then clean up."

"You don't need to. It's only a tiny cut. I'll live." She bent and picked up the larger pieces, and he kneeled down beside her to get the rest. "Good thing it didn't shatter, but I'm sorry about the mess."

"It's fine. I've got this." He dumped the pieces of glass in the bin, then grabbed some paper towels to mop the floor.

Their faces were inches from each other and she held her breath, wanting him to kiss her so bad that she couldn't think straight. She prayed he didn't have any better sense. Just for one moment she wanted to feel his mouth on hers.

"Mila? You alright?"

She closed her eyes and licked her lips. "Chase. You better move away now. This mess is nothing compared to the way I'm feeling."

Before she could move his mouth came down on hers. Hard.

CHAPTER TWELVE

"I'm sorry. I shouldn't have done that." Chase stood up and wiped his mouth.

Mila backed into the corner between the counter and the fridge. "No, you shouldn't have but I'm still glad you did."

"Are you crazy? Why would you be glad?" He ran a hand through his hair with shaky fingers. His knees were weak and he wanted to pick her up, carry her into the bedroom, strip her naked, and kiss every available tantalizing inch. Those tight jeans of her outlined a perfectly shaped ass, and her Laker shirt did nothing to hide her luscious, grapefruit sized breasts. He couldn't wait to get his hands on them, and his mouth watered as he thought about sucking on those nipples.

He groaned and she smiled. What a crazy bitch. Didn't she know better?

"I'm glad because now we both know how bad we want it, and how hard it is not to give in." She put a hand on her throat, and took a couple of deep breaths. "Although sometimes I feel like we're fighting nature and delaying the inevitable, which really means we're delaying the very thing you are here to find out. The secret behind this place."

"So what are you saying?" He folded his arms over his chest and kept his distance. His bags were packed, should he run now while he still could?

"I'm not sure," she said sweetly. "A part of me thinks that we should spend the next night or two delving into this mystery, and really let things heat up. The other part of me thinks that is what this mysterious force wants and we'd be playing into its or her hand. Like that angel I was talking about, or Venus. Ouch," she said, rubbing at her chest. "What was that?"

"What was what?"

"I felt a sting in my chest," she said, looking worried. "Hurt like hell."

"I don't know. You didn't get a sliver of glass there, did you? Maybe I should look."

"No, you damn well shouldn't. I probably strained a muscle."

"Right. And back to this discussion--allowing things to heat up between us is the worst idea of all. We need to be scientific about this, and analyze all the information we have. I still firmly believe it's environmental and I aim to prove it."

"I think it's more romantic and emotional than that. Come on! Since when did anything in the water or the air make people fall in love?"

"I don't know, but we have to keep our heads on straight until we figure this out. The last thing we need is to be hopping into bed together."

"Then why did you kiss me?"

"Mysterious forces at work?" he said with a nonchalant grin, hiding he hoped, his physical awareness of her. Every nerve end was on alert, his pulse beat way too fast, and blood flowed through his veins ending in his crotch.

"You of all people should know better. Being so clinical and all."

"Your eyes were begging for a kiss."

"They were not." She pushed away from the counter. "Look, enough of this conversation. Obviously it's not going to be solved tonight, and I'm hungry as a horse."

She handed him a plate with the two seasoned steaks. "There's a grill on the porch. Think you can handle it?"

"I can handle it all right." He glanced at her breasts and ground his teeth. "Got a light out there?"

"Yup, it's behind the drapes, and you can go out the sliding glass door."

He turned on the light and looked out at the enclosed back yard. "Hey, this is really nice. You should have a dog, not a cat."

Her wooden porch was painted white and had room for the grill, a small table and a couple of chairs, and a slider-swing for two. If it were warmer, he might want to spend a little time in it with this foxy little lady, but thankfully it was damn cold.

He sized up her yard, noting a few fruit trees, a decent size lawn and a garden patch. "Apple trees?" he guessed. "And you grow your own vegetables?" Shook his head and gave her a quizzical look. "Didn't take you for the type."

"What type did you take me for?"

"I don't know. Not the earthy kind."

She laughed. "I'm a complex person. Don't bother trying to figure me out."

"If you say so." He turned on the grill. "How do you like your steaks?"

"Medium rare. More red than pink." She gave him a teasing smile. "Watch out for rats. The big ones like to come out at night."

Something ran over his toes and he jumped a damn foot. At her laugh he glanced down and saw it was Charlie. "You're a piece of work, you know that?"

"I do know." She poured herself another glass of wine and lifted it in his direction. "Hurry up. I'm hungry."

He closed the sliding glass door and stood near the grill to keep warm. He could have gone back inside for his jacket but decided he'd rather tough it out. He blew into hands and put them under his armpits to keep warm, watching and waiting for the meat to change color. When he was satisfied that they were cooked to perfection he removed the steaks and took them inside.

Last think he wanted was to keep a hungry woman waiting.

Especially this one who had a habit of looking at him like he would be her last meal.

The table was set, wine poured and she had a salad on the table and two baked potatoes with sour cream and butter. He slid the steaks on the two plates and washed his hands before sitting down.

"Looks good." He lifted his glass and toasted her. "Thanks for having me."

She smiled. "I'm not having you. Remember?"

He swallowed a good size lump in his throat. "Let's eat, and then try to get through the night. Don't make this anymore challenging than it already is."

She rubbed the spot on her chest. "Okay, okay, don't be so testy." She bit into the steak. "Damn this is good. Another one of your talents, I see. You're a savvy reporter who plays guitar. A handy man with a grill. What other hidden talents do you possess?"

She played with the stem on her glass of wine. Her face was looking flushed again.

He took a long sip from his glass, trying to figure out a way to distract her. "I'm a whizz at backgammon and not too shabby at chess." He cut into his steak, and took a bite, chewing slowly so he wouldn't have to talk.

Her fevered eyes met his. "I bet you do a lot of things well." She looked at his mouth and then her gaze traveled down. Lucky for him the table hid his lower half or she'd see how her words and hot glances affected him.

"I try. And right now I'm trying very hard to keep this conversation from taking a twist we'd later regret. Now eat your steak, and stop trying to entice me. It's a no go. Not going to work."

She laughed. "So you say, but I think differently. The night is young, and we'll see who has the stronger will."

"Why are you eager to mess with this thing? It can only bring us down. Control us like it does everyone else."

"I think we can use it. See the power, give in to it sexually and once abated we can then turn our full attention on solving the riddle." She smiled and picked up her glass of wine, stroking the stem with her long, slim fingers. "Then you can go back to your real life."

He refused to look at her. Why tempt fate any more than they already were? Besides, common sense had to prevail if they stood a fighting chance. "Let's put this conversation on hold. You've gotta know that your reasoning is unbalanced."

"Unbalanced? How dare you?" Her head snapped up, and her eyes were full of fire.

"Yes. You wouldn't be suggesting this if you were thinking clearly."

"Oh, what the hell do you know? I proposition men all the time. When I want to, of course. I don't sleep around, but I know pretty much all the available men in town and when I want some action, I usually let them know."

"So, that's how it works. You call the shots."

"Better believe it. So, this is nothing. Just makes sense, that's all." She licked her lips. "If we choose to do it, then we are in control. See? We aren't doing it because of some unknown force."

"Makes sense put like that." He cut off another piece of steak and jammed it in his mouth. "But, I don't like the idea. Not at all."

"What do you recommend we do to uncover the truth?"

"I suggest that after dinner we start our research—two computers, two brains going to work."

"It's a lot less fun," she said with a twinkle in her eye.

"A lot less dangerous you mean."

They finished their meal in silence, both lost in their own thoughts, and then Chase insisted on helping clear the table and putting the dishes away.

When the kitchen was back to normal he booted up his laptop and sat down at the table prepared to work. She sat at the other end of the table with her iPad, and he wondered what she was researching. He had already checked out the environmental aspect earlier today, but he wasn't ready to give up on it. Anything else was just too whimsical and he was a practical guy.

"Why are you looking at me?" She glanced up. "Get working. Although I think you're barking up the wrong tree. I know this area and there's never been any scandal about chemical wastes, or a cancer cluster. This sudden boom in the marital market is recently new—probably only in the last three, four years or so."

"That's encouraging, I guess. Maybe it's just people getting all worked up about nothing."

"Could be, but what about you and me? All this heated stuff going on? You're not even my type."

He pushed his chair back and stood up. "Like hell I'm not."

A smile lifted the corner of her mouth. Her eyes slid over him, one lazy eyeful at a time. "Not only would I have to be blind, but I'd also have to be thinking unclearly to be attracted to you." She cracked open the bottle of water next to her, and took a long slug. "Why are you looking at me like that?"

"I don't believe you." He took two steps in her direction then stopped. "You're just trying to provoke me, aren't you?" His eyes narrowed. "Is this a game to you?"

"Of course not." She wiped her mouth. "Once in a while, I must admit I feel some kind of pull. But it's got nothing to do with you, really. It's not personal. It's just this thing around here."

"I think it's got everything to do with me," he stepped closer, "and if you're not careful, I might just have to prove it."

CHAPTER THIRTEEN

Her heart raced. "Is that right? Wouldn't be very smart of you, now would it?" She gave him a wicked smile. He was only about a foot from her chair and she could hear him breathing hard, see the excitement in his eyes, feel the heat emanating from his skin.

Oh yes, this was going to be fun! She'd decided after the kiss in the kitchen that she was losing the battle, but sometimes that had to happen in order to win the war. Now to get him to her side so they could fight the common enemy.

After sex.

"Do you feel the pull now?" he asked, and put a hand on the back of her neck, his long fingers splayed in her hair as he massaged her scalp, making her squirm with delight.

She tossed her head back to look at him as tingles of pure pleasure shot through her system. "I feel something. It's nice."

"You like that? What about this?" He tugged her out of the chair and pulled her into his arms, capturing her mouth before she could answer.

He sucked the breath right out of her, kissing her so long and so deep that she could only cling to him and hope he didn't let go. Had she been inclined she could probably have pushed away but instead she wrapped a leg around his, effectively trapping him.

She opened her mouth, admitting his tongue to do whatever he liked. It swept inside to taste her, dived deep into her throat, and began a dueling dance with her own. She could hardly breathe, but who needed air?

Panting, she shifted ever so slightly, needing to get closer. She grabbed his shoulders, holding him firm, wanting more kisses, more tongue, more hands, more of him. She moaned his name.

"What are you feeling," he whispered. "Tell me."

"I'm feeling as though I'm floating on air, and there's a magnetic force pulling me into you and it's so strong that I'd die if it were broken." She spoke in a hoarse voice that sounded like a stranger's. "I need you."

"Could you say that a little louder?"

She tried to laugh, but the need in her was so great that tears sprang to her eyes instead. "No. Don't tease me. Please?"

"Mila. This is serious. Listen up." He pulled back to look at her. "I want you. Should I leave?"

"No, no, no. Stay, please stay. I want this, you, everything."

He took her head in his hands and looked directly into her eyes. "Are you sure? We don't have to do this. We can fight it. Together."

"No. I don't want to fight it. I want to give in. Just once. Please just once. We can know the enemy, then form a winning battle strategy. Later."

He stepped back and jammed his hands in his pockets. His eyes were wide and worried. "This is a really big mistake."

"Maybe yes, maybe no, but don't make me ask again. Please make love to me." She reached out a hand and touched his face, stroking the curve of his cheek. "I lied before. I am attracted to you and was the first time I saw you--before either one of us got bit."

He lifted an eyebrow. "You sure about that?"

"More sure than anything I've said since I met you."

He laughed softly. "I would have fallen for you if you'd been wearing a sack. Prettiest damn woman I've ever met." His eyes grew moist. "You in that wedding dress, wow, I wanted to buy the entire package."

She frowned. "Why are we talking? I told you what I want and I'm a very impatient woman."

"That's just one thing I like about you."

"You'll like more, I promise." She grabbed his hand. "Come with me and please don't freak out. We're both adults and we can make love if we want to. Our choice. No one else's." She gave a short little laugh. "Certainly not Venus's or any damn angels."

She felt a little pang in the region of her chest and rubbed it absently. "My heart ache's for wanting you." The words were out of her mouth before she could stop them, but she knew they were true.

"Well, we better do something about that, shouldn't we?"

"We should." She led him to her bed, turned down the sheets, and gave a shiver of expectation. "I'm going to the bathroom for a minute. Please be naked when I get back."

"Don't be long. I want to undress you."

When she returned he was under the covers, his chest bare, sitting up with his elbow supporting his head. He looked adorable, sexy, and edible lying there waiting for her. She grinned and waved the condoms in her hand.

"Play time." She pounced on the bed. "We have "glow in the dark" condoms which are completely safe, or flavored—strawberry and chocolate. Then we have these studded beauties designed to enhance our mutual pleasure."

He looked at the handful. "You come prepared." He picked one out. "The men in Serendipity must be lined up at your door."

"No. No line. I sell these in my shop so I brought home a little selection just in case we couldn't keep our hands off each other."

"Well, in the name of research, we might have to try each one." He pulled her down and began to kiss her in earnest. His hand slipped under her shirt and found her breast. She arched into him, needing his loving.

"I've been waiting to touch these since I saw them popping out of that gown." He bent his head, lifted her top and blew hot breaths on her nipples through the lacy bra. "You are so beautiful. Sit up so I can take your top off. I need to see them, taste them."

She sat up, and he pulled it over her head and unfastened her bra. His eyes feasted and her nipples peaked.

He filled his hands with her plump breasts and didn't seem to mind that they were bigger than she liked. "Beautiful, so so beautiful." He took one of her nipples in his mouth and sucked gently, then lathered it with his tongue, while his other hand continually stroked the other.

She moaned his name, pushing herself further into his mouth. "Jeez, Chase, don't stop."

"Never." He licked and kissed her then flipped her over onto the bed. He slipped out from under the sheets and pulled her jeans down her legs, tossing them to the floor. She was left with nothing but her underwear and a cavernous craving inside of her.

He spread her legs and his mouth found her warm center. He pushed the lacy fabric aside and touched and stroked her, kissing her through the light fabric until she couldn't take it anymore.

"The condom. Where is it?"

"Not yet. I need to taste you first." He removed her panties and slipped his tongue inside the heated, convulsing core of her. "Gentle," he said. "We have all night and I'm not going anywhere but here."

Her first explosion came fast and furious, and when she could breathe again she called out his name. "Chase. You better put that condom on, because I'm coming to get you."

"Yes, ma'am. In times like these, I don't mind a bossy dame."

CHAPTER FOURTEEN

Chase was above all things a pretty basic guy with lots of girlfriends behind him and more to look forward to in future. He enjoyed sex as much as the next guy, and experimented some too, but when it came to sheathing himself he'd only used Trojan Magnum lubricated for the ease and fit. Since it worked and had a solid reputation behind it, he didn't bother to improvise.

Holy crap!

What the hell was going on inside this thing? Mila had tossed aside his glow in the dark pick and handed him the studded one, with a promised whisper that he'd like it. Like it, hell! How was he going to be able to perform like a man lucky enough to be inside this beautiful woman and make it last, when his pleasure zone was aroused beyond control?

She was moaning and tossing her head, so obviously she was enjoying it too, but hell, he wanted to experience every inch of her and take his own sweet time doing it. This two sided studded condom was acting like a vibrator and driving them both over the edge.

Hold on, buddy, he told himself and gritted his teeth. Between the damn love bug and this damn vibrating sheath he was about to blow his load like some horny teenaged kid.

He opened his eyes and looked down at Mila's beautiful pink face. Her eyes were sweetly glazed over and her mouth was wet and panting. She looked so damn hot. He played with her breasts as he drove himself deep inside. Nothing in life had ever been sweeter, and if this was to be the end of him, let it be. He could die in her arms one very happy man.

Who needed dreams and ambitions about going off to a war, when he could get this heady excitement right here? Doing live reports in Syria or South Sudan couldn't possibly compare to this kind of bliss. He pounded harder and Mila lifted her hips to match him thrust for thrust. Or Libya. Iraq? No fucking way.

He closed his eyes, imagining the guerilla warfare instead of focusing on this mind blowing erotic experience he was sharing with delicious Mila—trying to be heroic and keep his loins from exploding.

"Yes, yes, yes," she screamed and he knew she was coming.

He gave one last thrust and poured himself into her, then collapsed breathing as hard as if he'd climbed a mountain top. He laced his fingers through hers, and put his head on her chest. Her breathing was as uneven as his.

"You okay? Want me to get off?" He shifted slightly so he could kiss the breast closest to him.

"Not unless you have to. I like you just where you are."

He was still inside of her, and it felt warm, protected, and he was in no hurry to leave this particular place. She liked it and he did too. Maybe they had more in common than he'd originally thought.

"Never had an experience like that before. Not sure about all that stimulation. I nearly lost it too soon."

"You did just fine," she answered and kissed the top of his head.

He lifted his head to look at her. "That's it?

"What do you want? An award?" She nipped his shoulder. "Okay. You did better than fine. It was spectacular. Happy?"

He grinned. "Kind of. Not really. Now that we know how good it is, how are we going to stop?"

"We just will, that's all. Mind over matter."

"I have a mind right now to do you again and again until you can't walk straight."

"Oh, is that right?" Her hands moved down his back and cupped his ass. "So who's stopping you? I might as well get my money's worth if one night is all there is."

He didn't answer. Instead he captured her mouth in a long hungry kiss that had them both breathless and panting for more. He rolled off her, grabbed another condom and went right back to where he wanted to be.

They took it slow, one delicious thrust at a time. He flipped her over so she'd be on top and took her breasts in his hands. Her head was thrown back, her eyes were closed and he'd never seen a more beautiful woman in his life. Already he knew it would be hard leaving her, but nevertheless he would.

If she wanted to come with him to San Francisco or around the world, he wouldn't say no, but staying in Serendipity Falls was not the place he intended to end up. It was too small for him. There wasn't a newspaper or a TV station in town. What would a journalist do all day?

He stopped thinking and surrendered to the moment. It might take him a few days to uncover the truth around this place and until he did he would give Mila some good loving for as long as she'd let him.

* * *

Mila had been truthful about her sex life. When she wanted more than just dinner she'd let a man know, but here in Serendipity there were few men who interested her and filled her with desire. It just didn't happen so she lived pretty much a nun-like existence.

Well, she had never really known how good it could be or exactly what she'd been missing. Heck, if sex could be this incredible all the time, she'd sign up on the dotted line.

With her eyes closed, she gave into the pleasure, rocking gently back and forth, allowing the moment to build and build. She didn't want to climax, not yet, she wanted to savor the moment for as long as she could, not knowing when there would be another chance to have this mind blowing experience again.

He filled her in ways she'd never imagined. She felt him fully inside of her, touching her in places she'd never been touched before. It was more than sexual, she felt him everywhere as though he had captured her heart and soul. It didn't scare her the way it should. It was all right. For this moment she wouldn't fight the powers that be, but surrender and enjoy it for all it was worth.

Chase had come into her life for a reason. She believed that, just as she believed in karma and God and the ever-after. She didn't think Chase's arrival was divine intervention, but he was here so she could learn something about herself. Perhaps it was to make her see that her brothers were right—there was more to life than just work. She deserved more. Life was richer with someone to love.

She rocked harder, realizing how precious this moment was. Having someone fill her inside and out, making her feel whole, and opening her to a world of possibilities was way more than she'd expected, more than she had hoped for.

She opened her eyes and bent to kiss Chase softly on the lips. His eyes flew open and filled with tenderness. She linked hands with him, and moved slowly, never breaking eye contact, wanting to share this beautiful experience in its entirety with this very special man.

He seemed to understand and kept pace with her. His eyes were warm and loving and she knew he was sharing the richness of this mating, and that he got the fact that for whatever reason right now, in this time and place, they were meant to be together. For how long she wasn't sure. But it was meant to be.

As a practical, non-romantic person, this belief should have been a huge stretch for her but she accepted it without question. And found a certain amount of peace in that.

"You are driving me crazy, girl," he whispered, taking hold of her hips. He moved her quicker, took her deeper, held her sweeter, and kissed her longer than any man ever had or ever could.

For this moment only, she felt love seeping from her body to his. She wasn't afraid because she had the will, the power to let it be so.

Later, much later, they stumbled out of bed and showered together. They didn't talk about what happened between them, because words were redundant. They knew their relationship had substantially changed, but their future remained the same.

When Chase got his story, he would leave. And Mila might see the world a little differently, and forgive herself for the sins of her past.

CHAPTER FIFTEEN

Chase woke up, not on the sofa but warm and snug in Mila's bed. The sleeping arrangement had only made sense after making love for half the night and neither of them had wanted to separate themselves.

They were in this together. And may benevolent forces treat them kindly for he was a goner through and through. He'd never met a woman like Mila before and he doubted that if he scoured the earth and back, he ever would. He didn't think it had anything to do with the Serendipity magic either. She was a woman that was damn well impossible not to love.

Even if she was a huge pain in the ass. She had pushed him off her around two o'clock in the morning and had sent him to his side of the bed. He'd hoped to keep her wrapped in his arms and cuddle with her until dawn but she had a mind of her own when it came down to sleeping side by side. She'd silently consented to playing toesies with him, but that had been the only part of him she'd allowed near her when it came time to sleep. Well, poor sucker that he was, he'd taken that small token of comfort.

But now he had a throbbing dick and no place to put it. He'd heard Mila taking a shower and had slipped out of bed to sneak in with her, but found the bathroom door locked. What the hell? Thinking of her wet and naked and locked away from him was pure torture.

He padded into the kitchen and made the coffee, then came back into her bedroom and sat on the edge of the bed. Naked as the day he was born, he sat and waited for the door to open.

She came out with a towel wrapped around her head and a thick terry cloth robe concealing that magnificent body of hers. She grinned when she saw him.

"Hey. You're awake."

"You locked the door. The shower woke me and I hoped you might let me in." He stood up and it was obvious that every part of him had hoped for the same thing.

She glanced down, then slowly let her eyes slide over him before returning to his face. "I see." Her cheeks grew pink. "You look a little frisky this morning."

"Got a hard-on so big that a cat can't scratch it." He glanced down at himself then back up at her. "I think we should get rid of a little more friction between us so it can burn itself out."

"Oh, you do, do you?" She pulled her underwear out of a drawer. "I think we should be grateful that we had one terrific night together and not keep stroking the fire."

"I want you to stroke *my* fire." He moved swiftly and turned her around to face him. He undid the belt of her robe and let it fall away. With greedy hands he pushed the robe open and drank in his fill.

126

"I want to touch you," he said gently, "but it's your call."

She didn't say a word, not for several long, painful seconds, then her voice came out higher than its norm. "I don't think we should, but I'm not going to stop you either. If you think you can handle it and still walk away when your job is done, well, I'm sure I can too."

"Oh, Mila." His hands slipped inside her robe and pulled her up against him. His cock rubbed against her belly and found a small amount of relief. He wanted her bad enough to promise her the world and to make it happen.

"Touch me, Mila. And come back to bed." His mouth found a sweet spot on her neck and he kissed her lightly, then nibbled on the lobe of her ear.

She took him in her hand and he shuddered with pleasure. "I will make this right for you. As much as you want, whatever you need. I won't hurt you, I promise."

He kissed her deeply, tasting the minty flavor of her toothpaste, the clean, sweet, lovely taste of this woman he desired, and was filled with need. He had to taste so much more of her that he'd forgotten during the heady passion of last night.

He took her by the hand and gently pushed her on the bed, spreading her legs so he could feast. His tongue ran up and down the inside of her thighs and she quivered and sucked in a breath.

"Don't worry. I'll take it slow."

"Chase. I'm not used to this. I don't know if I'm okay or not."

"Trust me. Do you trust me, Mila?"

She nodded her head and tears blurred her eyes.

"With my whole heart."

That was all he needed to know, and he put his hands under her delicious rump and lifted her for better access. His tongue explored the fresh clean taste of her then needed to dive deeper. He held her and sucked on the sweet flesh, finding that special little nub that made her cry out and cling to him, begging for more.

When she bucked and shuddered and found her release, he heard his name cried out. With a heart too full and emotions too deep, he swept her into his arms and kissed her tenderly.

"Whatever happens to us, I just want you to know that it was worth it," he said, tucking a lock of hair behind her ear. "I've never met anyone like you and it has nothing to do with a love bug either. It's just you, Mila. I would have felt this way if we'd met anywhere."

She smiled but tears slid down her cheeks. "How do we know? This probably wouldn't have happened anywhere else. We'd have glanced at each other and walked away. You know that neither of us wants a commitment, we have too much to do."

"True, but for the other couples out there I'm going to carry on my research. I intend to find something, bring it back, and show you and the rest of the world that there is a sane, scientific reason for this activity."

"Okay. You do that." She swiped at her tears. "I would like to think our emotions are real and not manifested by some unknown force."

"I promise you they are not."

"Oh! I do so like you, I do."

She slipped away from him long enough to pull another condom from her bedside drawer, and spent the next hour showing him various sides of like.

For a woman who didn't get around much, she certainly knew her way around him, and if he wasn't careful he'd be sucked in too deep and never find his way home.

Not that he had a whole lot waiting for him. His mother lived outside the city in the Tri-Valley area and he made a point of visiting her a few times a week. She had someone come in each day to help her but eventually the Alzheimer's would get worse and she'd have to move into assisted living. By that time, she'd barely recognize him or remember him if she did. He had a few friends, mostly guys he hung around with from the surf club where he spent his free hours. They'd go for beers and burgers once in a while but wouldn't miss him for a minute if he were gone. There'd been a nice girl in his life until around six months ago. She'd wanted more than he was willing to give her, and so he had set her free. Actually, she'd told him she wanted a ring by Christmas or she was through, and he had bought her a gift certificate for a day at the spa and a Coach handbag, thinking that was a better alternative.

She'd left his house in tears, and he'd felt really bad for a day or two, ruining her Christmas and all her dreams and everything, but he knew it was better for both of them if he didn't call again. By New Year's she'd hooked up with someone else and he heard just the other day that they were engaged.

Mila was a different breed of woman. Independent, strong, feisty, and quite unforgettable. It might have been a whole lot smarter if he'd stayed clear and had found a hotel in Serendipity Falls to spend a few nights, but smarter wasn't necessarily better. And he'd be damned if he would regret a minute of this.

When she took her second shower, he poked around her kitchen and busied himself by cooking her breakfast. Bacon sizzled and the scrambled eggs were nearly done when she snuck up behind him and wrapped her arms around his middle. She nuzzled her cheek into his back, and he felt a large lump grow in his throat.

He was still in his boxers, waiting to shower, but he turned around and drew her in, enveloping the warmth, the enticing, invigorating woman in his arms. "I made breakfast," he whispered, fighting the urges inside of him.

"I see." She kissed him lightly then slipped out of his arms and nabbed a slice of bacon, devouring it in quick bites. "Sexy and a good cook. I will have to recommend you to all the lovely ladies who come to my shop. You're definitely a keeper."

She said it in jest, but she might as well have used a sword--it cut into him just the same. Her eyes glittered with unshed tears and he could see that her flippant remark had cost her dearly too.

"I'm not interested," he said and took her face into his hands and kissed her mouth softly. "Go sit down. Breakfast will be ready in a minute."

"Okay. I'll grab my coffee and get out of your way." She poured cream in her cup, filled it with the rich, dark fragrant coffee, and sat at the table.

Mila was dressed for work in her black slacks, pink turtleneck sweater and a fur-lined vest that didn't hide her womanly curves. She was a full blossomed woman, and he wanted to peel everything off her and take her back to bed, but that was just crazy—Serendipity crazy, so he turned back to the stove, removed the bacon and eggs and buttered the toast.

He served them both, then sat down next to her, and did his best to ignore the hairy beast of a cat that slithered between his ankles.

"Charlie—go eat your own food," Mila said absently, and crumbled some bacon to hand feed the cat.

They ate their meal is silence, content to be quiet and lost in their thoughts. Too much talking couldn't make anything right and they both knew what they had to do so it was pointless anyway.

She did the dishes while he showered and dressed. He cleared the mirror above the sink and began to shave. When his face was smooth, he patted an aftershave on his cheeks then went into the living room, his eyes searching for Mila.

His breath caught in his throat as he watched her standing next to the patio door peering out the window. It was nothing, he told himself. Mila was checking out the weather, a bright and glorious day. A beautiful woman taking in a beautiful day.

Nothing to get choked up about.

They'd slept together once. Known each other only a few days. Their situation might be new and unusual, but he had to admit it was far from casual.

After he dropped Mila off at work, Chase felt a little emptiness inside. He wondered how it was going to feel leaving her, even though his head told him they'd both be better off. But when he drove away he knew it would take more than a few days to forget.

CHAPTER SIXTEEN

Chase drove down to the falls and decided to do a little digging around, scratching the surface of what he hoped to find. To be honest, he didn't have a clue what he expected to discover and his research on-line hadn't offered any ideas either. Perhaps it was to justify his paycheck or to fill in a few hours before seeing Mila again. Maybe it was an attempt to push her out of his mind. Damn woman had no right to be there in the first place. No woman ever had—how had she crept in?

When he solved this mystery, which he damn well would, he hoped to regain control of his emotions—but if it turned out to actually be a love bug, he'd kick its ass for infecting him and Mila and all the other mindless, deliriously happy couples this way.

He parked in the lot then headed down the path where he'd sat with Mila yesterday, and stepped over the broken limb that had fallen out of the sky and nearly cracked their skulls. He glanced up and saw the tree, moving quickly in case another branch was about to fall. Didn't want to get killed out here, getting infected was enough of a worry.

He walked for another ten minutes and came to a stream which led down to the lake. He wasn't sure if he could get anywhere near the falls, or what he expected to find if he did. But it was a warm, sunny day, and he didn't have anything better to do. Perhaps with some miracle from above he might actually discover something. A man could hope, and if nothing else, Chase still had plenty of that.

He followed the stream, picked his way through underbrush and climbed over some rocks, then stopped when he reached the lake. It was so clear he could see the small smooth stones on the bottom, and fish as they quickly darted by. It was an inspiring sight with the mountain and the falls as a backdrop. It evoked dreams of grandeur and had his blood pumping.

He thought about the panhandlers that had first come here so many years ago, filled with child-like hope and excitement that for most quickly turned into despair. Fortunes won and fortunes lost, but for one shiny moment in history strangers from afar were connected by one common goal. To find gold. To get rich. To live the American Dream.

Tired from the marathon night he'd spent in Mila's bed, and the challenging walk from the path to the lake, he jumped up on one of the boulders to sit for awhile. He leaned back so he could stare up at the sky, and remembered some of the things he'd learned from his recent research. A carpenter from New Jersey had been working to build a water-powered sawmill near Sacramento when he found a few flakes of gold at the base of a mountain. He'd known right then and there that it was gold for sure. Days after his discovery the Mexican-American war ended and California belonged to the United States. Word got out about the gold quickly, and newspapers revealed the location at Sutter's Mill.

People from San Francisco left their jobs to search for gold, migrants arrived in boats from as far away as Hawaii and China. People borrowed money, mortgaged their property and spent their life savings making the difficult journey. Many left families behind, and the women held the responsibility to run their farms or businesses and raise the children. Gold mining towns sprung up all over the place, bringing crime and chaos with it. Meanwhile, San Francisco became a thriving metropolis, perhaps a beacon at the end of a tunnel.

Just as quickly as it came, the good news, the excitement and glitter of gold dried up. But what about Serendipity Falls? Chase wondered. He sat up and glanced around, filled with a new energy. There was indeed a story to be told, and he could feel it all the way inside his journalist bones. As sure as the carpenter from New Jersey, he knew there was a nugget of gold that he needed to extract and pass along to the people. This was his story, his future and his good fortune.

Something magical was happening here and it might not bring material wealth but it certainly drove people to leave their homes in search of a happier life. His job was to discover and report the mystery.

CUPID

A story! A story! I must help this dear boy find his wonderful story, but oh, what will he tell? For there is only one truth and that must never be told. Still, he is a clever young man with a very good heart and Mila loves him dearly. We must keep him here, mustn't we? Oh, yes, for I fear that if her heart is broken, little Mila will never risk it again. And that won't do. No, it won't do at all.

I'm in the love making business, and it doesn't make me money or bring me fame, but it does transcend my soul. It also fills me with pride.

So, let me put my mind to work. I must help Chase discover something wonderful, so good in fact that he will win respect and recognition enough to make him a satisfied man. Mila will do the rest, I'm sure, if last night was any example. Who ever knew there were so many plastic things that could bring couples such joy? If I weren't a Cupid I might want to be in that condom business, for sure.

But that's not my worry--it's providing a clue for Chase. Perhaps I need to take a look around.

Dusting off my wings, I set sail into the air. It's been quite some time since I've flown this high and I fear that I might faint. But oh, just a little higher. I want to see beyond the falls, and not fall in it.

I puff and pant and flap for all I'm worth, and yes, I do see the mountain and the spot where the waterfall begins. Out of breath, I swish down and land right above the crevice and find a rock to sit for a few minutes. I gulp in air, and wait for my breathing to get under control. Don't want to have a heart attack, now do I?

If I died, my nephew might move in and in his clumsy way he might destroy all that I've worked for and tried to achieve. He has a good heart, but he's young and not the most clever Cupid on the planet. Still, I do not want him to leave his home in Vegas and take over my territory. This is my home, my people and I must live and protect them for a great many more years. At least another three to four hundred will do.

But enough about me. I'm fine, and I have a job to accomplish.

As I glance around a sense of peace overcomes me. I understand. It all begins here. The mystery of Serendipity Falls must be discovered in this very spot.

Oh, my, but what is that?

I jump down from the mighty big rock to inspect something unique and much more impressive. I see a crater. Something created this enormous hole behind the falls. A meteor perhaps or an asteroid—something bigger than me fell from the sky and cracked open this mountain, leaving a message behind.

My reporter friend might very well have an interesting story to tell after all. Now I have to figure out a way to lead him here.

CHAPTER SEVENTEEN

Mila had an interesting day filled with a deluge of exuberant, eager, excitable brides, and she dealt with them all in her usual breezy, off-beat style that people seemed to relate to. But something was different today. She couldn't stop smiling. Or squeezing her knees together, reliving the night of sex she'd enjoyed with a man little more than a stranger. Yet she felt as though she'd known him forever. And trusted him completely.

Do all these happy couples feel that way?

If so, no wonder they were tripping over themselves to rush to the altar. She could understand it now. She didn't want to join the parade, but she could sit on the sidelines and watch with a heart filled with pleasure. She knew the giddiness of love and the strength of desire they experienced for now she shared it too. This added benefit would make her a much better wedding planner/business owner/dream maker, than she ever was before.

It was all good.

Or was until Devon pranced in. Mila couldn't help but notice that her handsome brother was still a babe magnet, for the moment he entered the young ladies in her shop gaped openly at him and conversation stopped.

"He's taken ladies," she called out, and gave her brother a kiss on the cheek. "You better wear a sign around your neck."

"I'm not interested, and aren't these woman supposed to be buying wedding gowns or something?" He gave a quick glance around, then flushed as all eyes were upon him.

Mila didn't really blame them, for Devon was just an all-round hunk. Six foot two, big shoulders to lean on, sexy cleft in his chin, dark wavy hair and flashing blue eyes.

"So what brings you here?" she asked, linking arms with him and pulling him aside.

"You. Kyle told me that there's a guy hanging around you and he thinks the two of you are smitten." He winked. "Figured you might want some advice."

"Smitten or bitten?" she asked with a grin. "Kyle's right, but no advice needed. I know what I need to do."

"Really? And what is that? You planning on marrying the guy?"

"No, I'm not planning anything. Heck, I have enough weddings to plan, including yours."

"Well, if you and this guy—what's his name, by the way?"

"Chase. Chase Carlton and he's a news reporter. From San Francisco."

"Okay, if you and this Chase guy are anything like Tara and me, well, there's not much use in fighting it. You might be able to delay things some, but what will be, will be."

"Sounds like a song." She laughed and gave his arm a squeeze. "You should see your face. You've got that worried look on." She shook her head. "It's okay. It really is. We've got a handle on it. And he's going to leave in a few days."

"Yeah, you sure about that?" Devon shuffled his feet, and looked down at the floor. "I can't believe you're not freaking out. How do you know he'll leave?"

"He has no choice. His job's in San Fran. He's leaving as soon as he gets his story. Right now, he's trying to uncover the truth about Serendipity Falls, to prove that it's an environmental issue, or find a logical explanation."

"This is romance and love we're talking about. How could the environment or anything darn well logical possibly be involved? When it comes to the heart, there is no logic." He shifted his gaze to hers. "Trust me, I know."

"Yup, you do." She shrugged. "I agree with you in theory. Heck, I know it's mostly emotional, but there has to be a little logic, doesn't there? I mean we wouldn't fall for someone who wasn't our type."

"Not sure about that, at least not here in Serendipity. This place has become an epidemic, and we all should be quarantined." He looked out the window, pointing to the foot traffic. "Not that I'm complaining. I love Tara madly. But that's half the problem. It is mad."

She giggled. "I love you. You know that?"

He grinned. "See what I'm talking about? Love surrounds us." He winked. "That's really the reason I'm here. I want to meet this guy who has claimed your heart."

"You want to check him out, you mean." She frowned. "And I didn't say he's claimed anything."

"Right. Well, he still might be trying. Besides, you're my only sister and I don't want just anyone running off with you."

"No one's running off with me for starters. I'm not going anyplace." She looked around and lowered her voice, "This is a virtual gold mine and I'm not giving it up until the well runs dry."

"Don't blame you for that." He nodded as a couple of potential customers stopped looking at the window display and entered. "Here's more."

"And they'll be more behind them," she answered.

"Exactly." His voice filled with concern. "When was the last time you had a day off? Why don't you hire some part-time help or a manager so you can get a life?"

"I thought you didn't want me to get a life," she retorted. "At least not with Chase. And wait 'til you meet him. You'll love him too."

"When are you seeing him again?"

"In about an hour. He's picking me up." She chewed her bottom lip and didn't look at him when she spoke. "He's staying at the house. Just for a couple of days."

"Your house?"

"Of course, my house."

"Are you out of your frickin' mind?" he said in an overly loud voice, causing the customers to stop shopping and look in their direction.

141

"We can talk about this later. I have to get back to work. Come for dinner tonight. You can meet him then."

"Okay. Is your key still hidden where it usually is?"

"Yup. Make yourself at home. We will see you in an hour or two." She lifted her chin and looked him in the eye. "He's alright. You'll see."

"You've only known him for a few days."

"How long did it take you to realize that Tara was something special? Not that I'm saying he is."

"About a minute."

"So there you go." She turned him around and gave him a push toward the door. "Get the heat on and don't drink all the wine."

"I might need something stronger than that."

She laughed and watched his back until he closed the door, then turned to her customers. "Okay, ladies. That was my brother who's getting married in two weeks. Now, who needs assistance? The store will be closing in exactly one hour."

Once her satisfied customers left the store with their shopping bags in hand, Mila locked up and called Chase on his cell.

He answered right away. "Hey, good looking. What's up?"

"I closed early, and have a surprise waiting for you at home."

"You. Naked in bed?" he guessed.

"Not even close." She grinned and wished she could stop smiling so much. She was going to get premature wrinkles for sure.

"Condoms? In every shape and color?"

"Keep hoping."

"Uh. I give up."

"You give up too easily," she answered. "And you'll never guess so I might as well tell you. It's my brother, Devon. The one who's marrying Tara in two weeks."

"He's at the house? What do you want me to do? Get a hotel for the night?"

"No silly. Kyle told him about you and now he wants to meet you. That's all. I told him you were staying with me for a couple of days and then you'd be heading back to San Francisco. He's cool with it."

"He's a guy and you're his kid sister. He's not cool."

"You don't know him. And he can't say a word. After all, he knows first hand how this bug thing works."

"Oh great. He knows that part too? About us?"

"Yeah. Kyle told him. What was I supposed to do? Deny it?"

"Might have been the wisest thing. Now he's probably waiting for me with a shotgun in his hand."

"You wuss. He doesn't have a shotgun, and neither do I. So you're safe. You can always hide behind my skirts if you're afraid."

"You're not wearing a skirt," he said with a laugh.

"So how many boxes should I bring home?"

"What kind of boxes?"

"Condoms, of course. Tell me, which was your favorite?"

"Don't you dare! We walk in with those things, he'll probably kill us both."

"Don't be so melodramatic. He's a lover, not a killer. At least he is now, after meeting Tara."

"And before that?"

"Lady killer."

Chase chuckled. "Okay, I'll man up and meet him. But that means you'll have to uncover the truth and write this story if something bad happens to me."

"I'll chance it." She glanced at her watch. "Did you find anything today?" Her stomach jumped. What would she say if he did? How would she feel? It was an unnerving thought. She had always been the one to leave, and she preferred it that way.

"No, but I'm on to something. I'm going back there tomorrow."

"Where?"

"The falls. It's where the story begins. Call it a journalist's hunch, but I have this gut feeling."

"Oh, well, that's great then, isn't it?" She tried to sound upbeat, even forced a smile on her stiff lips, but the happiness she'd felt all day had floated away. In an instant.

"I'm about ten minutes from the mall. Why don't you meet me at the Sears entrance?"

"Fine. I'll do that."

"Something wrong?" he asked quietly.

"No. Everything's perfect." She swiped a tear from the corner of her eye. She needed to buck up. Fast.

"Good then. I've missed you today," he added.

Her heart hammered, and a thrill rushed through her. "You were in my thoughts too."

"Damn shame, isn't it?"

"What is?" She tried to hold back all the wishes and wants and feelings that were struggling inside. They were both between a rock and a hard place. To love or not to love? To give up their individual needs in order to unite as one? Would that make either of them happy? She didn't think so.

"Us. Wanting to be together. Not wanting to be together. I mean, it's not an easy choice, is it?"

"Sure it is. We made our choice. Now we have to stick to the plan."

"Like that works!" He chuckled. "What about the decision not to go anywhere near each other? We made a pact that we weren't going to make love. How long did that last?"

"Yeah, well, this is different. This is about freedom. About doing what we want to do, not being controlled by outside forces."

"You might be right. It's just going to be difficult to let you go."

A lump formed in her throat and she couldn't speak.

When she could, she muttered, "I'm nearing the exit. See you in a minute."

"Looking forward to it."

CHAPTER EIGHTEEN

Chase didn't want to spend a night tip-toeing around Mila's brother, but he'd play nice for as long as he could. If he had a sister, and she looked and smelled and enticed anything like Mila, he'd want to stand bodyguard too. He probably had more in common with this big brother than he realized, but still, what was a man to do? Wasn't his fault he wanted to get naked with the guy's sister, and wanted to do unmentionable things to her every minute of the day.

He just hoped those impulses weren't clear on his face. If they were he probably only had a short time to live and didn't need to worry about his feelings or getting a story, or leaving her for good. Mila's brother might relieve him from all that.

He took several breaths and glanced toward the entrance of the mall, waiting for Mila to appear. His pulse raced as he eagerly waited.

This was ridiculous, he told himself. He'd never had such a reaction to a woman and he was smart enough to know that partly his giddiness was due to the magic of Serendipity Falls. The rest was all her. He'd told her the truth when he'd said he'd have fallen for her anytime, anyplace.

Maybe when he returned to the city, his apartment and his job, maybe he wouldn't have this hunger inside of him. The urge to take this woman into his arms and into his bed and keep her there for as long as they might live.

His blood thickened and warmed as his eyes met hers and she smiled in greeting. He leaned across the console and opened the door. She slid in and her smile faltered. He noticed her eyes were suspiciously bright as though hiding tears. Her cheeks were rosy and her pretty mouth trembled.

He gave her a quick kiss, wanting so much more, but knowing he had to be cautious. Couldn't show up at her house, with her looking ravished. That would be a recipe for disaster. He needed to show restraint.

"Are you nervous?" he asked, taking her chin into his hand. "I'll be a perfect gentleman around your brother and keep my hands off you." He grinned. "Let's just hope he doesn't stay long."

"I am a little concerned. Not because I have anything to hide from Devon, and we already talked about you, but because he knows even better than we do what kind of power this place holds." She grabbed his arm. "Did you find anything up at the falls? Are you any closer to finding out what this is?"

"No, but I will. I know it." His eyes drifted over her face, wanting to memorize every detail in lest he forget. "There's something up there, and I intend to find it."

She gnawed on her bottom lip. "I have mixed feelings about that. I wish I didn't, but I do."

"It's mutual, baby." He turned away, started the car, and headed out of the parking lot. "Let's not think about it for now. We need to get through tonight and the next few days. I'm sure everything will sort itself out."

"That's true. No point in worrying about something we can't fix."

"Besides, after I leave doesn't mean we can't see each other again. We could still see each other weekends and take it slow. See where it goes."

"I suppose, except that I work weekends too."

"Maybe you need to hire an assistant," he told her, eyes on the road.

"That's what my brother suggested."

Aha. Another thing they had in common. He might like this older brother after all. "What else did he tell you?"

"That we might not be able to fight this. He tried and failed."

"He's not us. And they both lived here, right? It's different because your job is here and mine is a couple of hundred miles away. Distance is a very negative factor when it comes to relationships. We would have to work hard to keep it."

She glanced out the side window, and he saw her wipe away a tear. He put his hand on her leg and gave it a squeeze. "You want me. I'm yours."

She sniffed and darted a look at his face. "You say that now but what if you do get a foreign assignment? Then we'd be talking a major conflict."

"Let's shelve this conversation for now. Tell me about your brother."

"Devon. Well, when he was twenty-one he had a shot at the Winter Olympics in Salt Lake City, but then he sprained an ankle two weeks before the event. He continued to compete but had to wait another four years for the next Olympic games. By that time he was twenty-five and knew he wouldn't get another chance. He was chosen by the US ski and snowboard federation and went to Turin, Italy, but never got to compete."

"What happened?"

"Crashed and burned on a practice run."

"Shit."

"That about sums it up." She was silent for a few minutes. "It was all he ever wanted, and he worked so hard all the way through school, giving up friends and fun to practice and ski hours every day. He's still my hero," she said simply.

"I bet he is." He winked at her. "I look forward to meeting him."

"Good. You'll like him, as long as you don't antagonize him too much."

"What? Like kiss you silly in front of him?"

She smiled. "That might do it."

"I'll try my best to stay away from you. But it won't be easy."

He pulled into the driveway and noticed the lights on. "He's already here?"

"Yes. He came into the shop around four. I didn't want him hanging around if he didn't need too."

He shot her a look. "Did you make the bed?"

She laughed. "Of course I did."

"What about the wrappers? Sheesh, they're probably all over the place."

"He won't go into my bedroom. Even brothers have off-limits."

He rubbed his jaw. "I hope so. Gawd—if he saw the evidence, he'd know exactly what I was doing with you all night long."

She laughed. "We'll know if he greets us with a shotgun at the door."

"Not funny," he grumbled.

"Sure it is." She bumped shoulders with him. "Come on, chicken. Lead the way."

"The moment he leaves I'm going to get you for that remark."

"Promise?" Her eyes danced and her mouth puckered in a kiss.

"As God is my witness."

"Okay, shush. Behave yourself." She linked arms with him and they walked in together. "He might be bigger than you, but if it came down to a fight, I think you'd be scrappier."

"Great. Thanks for the confidence boost."

Devon stood there, feet spread apart, arms folded and glared at Chase as if he knew all his secrets. He took his measure, then nodded and stepped forward.

"So you're the son-of-a-bitch who stole my sister's heart," Devon remarked.

Chase offered his hand and was surprised at the hearty handshake in return. "You know how it is around here. We didn't plan for this to happen."

Devon nodded. He looked from one to the other, as if unsure what to answer. Finally he said, "So what do you plan on doing about it? I know you have a job in the city, and Mila is tied up here. We wouldn't want her to leave."

Chase nodded. "I understand your concern, but to be honest, we haven't figured that out." He put an arm around Mila's waist and gave her a reassuring hug. "When we do, we'll be sure to let you know."

The big guy seemed to ponder that, and shot a serious look at his sister. "Guess that's fair. But I want to warn you. You hurt her and I'll break you in two."

Chase met him eye to eye, man to man. "Neither is going to happen, and I don't take kindly to threats."

Devon grinned. "Hell. I might like you after all." He walked into the kitchen. "I've got lasagna in the oven, and a good bottle of red open. Let's say we have a drink."

The evening went better than Chase could hope. They talked, they drank and enjoyed a good portion of the piping hot dish Devon had thoughtfully prepared.

"So what do you expect to find up at the falls?" Devon asked over a cup of coffee.

"I'll know it when I see it," Chase said solemnly. "But I have a feeling deep in my gut that there is something just waiting to be discovered, and that's why I'm here. To uncover the truth."

"I hope you do." He rubbed a hand over his face, then seemed to come to a decision. "I can probably get you a chopper if you want. I'm with the ski patrol and we have a few standing by. If something happens, that takes precedence, but if it's a quiet day, don't see why one of the pilots couldn't take you on a sightseeing mission. You're a journalist looking for a story. So why not?"

"That would be great, and the network would pay for his time."

"That's a deal then. I'll call you in the morning and make the arrangements."

"Appreciate it. I was hoping to get above the falls, but wasn't sure if there's an access road."

"Not much of one. This will be much easier." Devon glanced at Mila's face. "How about you? What if it is an environmental issue—how will that affect your business?"

"Not sure, but it won't change anything really. People will still flock here as long as romance continues to bloom. Doesn't matter what's causing this unusual state of affairs. As long as people are falling in love and rushing to the altar, our growth will continue and our community will thrive."

"True. Let's hope our residents have a great many more years of it. The happiness is spreading, and I for one never expected to find this kind of love." Devon laughed, "Wasn't long ago that I would have been ashamed to admit it, but now I'm proud as hell."

"That's really sweet," Mila said. "I wish Tara could hear you right now."

"I tell her all the time. She changed my life. For the better." He took their hands and clasped them together. "I hope it enriches yours too."

Chase gazed at Mila and something powerful passed between them. They might be reaching the point of no return, and yet Chase didn't fear it. Instead he was calmed.

CHAPTER NINETEEN

Mila walked her brother to his car, and kissed his cheek. "Thanks for coming tonight, and dinner and everything."

"My pleasure. I like him, Mila. Whether things work out between you or not, I know his heart is in the right place. That man loves you."

"Yes, well, we will see. He has ambitions, Dev. And what can a journalist do in Serendipity Falls? There isn't even a newspaper in town."

"Maybe he can start one."

"I hardly think so." She shrugged. "Give my love to Tara. Tell her to come in and be fitted for a dress. I have one that I think is perfect."

"I will. And you take care, ya hear?"

She smiled and waved him off, then returned inside to Chase. He was putting the dishes in the dishwasher, and she caught him scraping some of the sauce into Charlie's bowl.

"What are you doing?" she asked, watching the cat dive in. "He's already fat."

"Yeah, but he's our protector, remember? We need a big, beefy cat to keep the rats at bay. Besides he jumped up on the counter and tried to lick the plates. Figured this was a better option." He gave her hand a tug, and she stepped inside the circle of his arms. "Can I have my kiss now?"

"You can and you will. But first let me brush my teeth."

"Just one before you go?"

She put her arms around his neck and smacked his lips, then stayed to enjoy them a moment longer. "I missed kissing you tonight. I loved having Dev here, but all I wanted was to snuggle with you."

"Ditto, baby." He let her go. "Your brother is A-okay, but I was happy to see the back of him." He grinned. "And I say that in the nicest way."

She laughed. "He didn't overstay his welcome. I think he was in a hurry to get back to Mammoth and Tara."

"I'm sure he was. So what did he really think? About us, I mean?"

"What he said. He hopes we find our happiness too." She bit her lip and looked away. "But I don't want to keep you here anymore than you want to stay."

"That's not fair," he said, almost angrily. "My job is to report things out in the world, while yours is here. I wouldn't ask you to come with me. Not unless you wanted to, of course."

"No way. I love the mountains and this crazy small town. San Francisco is just too big and busy, and the traffic would scare me to death. Whenever I have to drive over the Golden Gate I get the heebie-jeebies."

"You'd get used to it in time."

"I don't have any inclination to get used to it. I'm happy here."

"Go brush. We will talk about this later. Much later. After I have my story and I'm ready to go."

"Okay. No point in worrying about it now. Not when I stuffed a few interesting packets in my handbag."

His eyebrows rose and his eyes danced underneath. "You are one incredible woman."

She put a hand on her hip and gave him a saucy smile. "Bet you say that to all the girls."

"No. Only one." He gazed at her for a long, heart thundering moment and she knew it was true. Devon was right. Chase loved her. He would leave just the same. And her life would go on as it had before—with only a small amount of pain. She'd miss him like crazy, but hard work would keep her busy. As it had in the past.

She brushed and flossed, then changed into a pair of Victoria Secret pajamas. Not sexy, but silky and comfortable, without restraints. She didn't want to be coy. Their time was limited and she wanted to enjoy every second they had.

She retrieved her handbag from the mudroom where she'd placed it when they came in, found her stash of condoms and ran over to Chase lounging on the sofa. She jumped on top of him and put her hands behind her back. "Pick one."

He reached for her left hand and she opened it, palm up. "What do we have here?" She grinned. "A flavored sampler pack. Banana or strawberry anyone?"

"What's in the other hand?"

"Boy, you are getting greedy, aren't you?" she teased, dropping the other box on his chest. "This is one of my top sellers, and I figured—what about us? Don't we deserve the best? I need to know what I'm selling, don't I?"

He glanced at the box and raised his eyes to meet hers. "A vibrating Johnny ring? I'm a little naive here--what exactly does it do?"

"It's used along with the condom and enhances the pleasure for both of us. Or we have another one waiting in my drawer next to the bed. For climax control. Speeds a woman up, slows a man down. We can do that one later."

He pulled her down and planted a big kiss on her lips. "I like the way you think."

"I like the way you kiss. And do all the other things."

His hands roamed over her, and fitted her butt. "Then what are we waiting for?"

"Not a thing." She kissed him long and slow and slipped her hands under his tee-shirt. She loved the firm muscles, the rippled six pack, the smooth texture of his skin. He was a beautiful man from his toes all the way upward. Not one thing about him would she change.

He put his hands under her pajama top and gently kneaded her breasts, playing with the nipples until they peaked in his hands. He lifted her top and kissed one.

She squirmed under him, wanting everything at once. Her hands went to his jeans, found his zipper and yanked it down. He was commando underneath. Her breath caught in her throat. "Oh. Damn. You should have warned me." She pulled him free and bent to lick him, teasing him with her tongue.

He was already hard and ready, pulsing with every flick of her tongue. The power was intoxicating, and she wanted this moment to last almost as much as she wanted it to end. He moaned her name and she lifted her mouth to quiet his with a searing kiss, then she returned to what she'd been doing.

She pushed his jeans down his legs, over his ankles, and cast them to the floor. She shoved his tee shirt high on his chest and straddled him for a moment, feasting her eyes. Then she bent and kissed him again. He sucked on a breast and she nearly lost it, then slid out of his grasp, and down his body to take him fully in her mouth.

He gasped and shook, but she didn't let go. Just once she wanted to taste him, to have him come without a condom separating them.

"No. Not like this," he tried to push her off, but she wasn't having it.

She broke away long enough to smile. "Yes. Like this." Then she went back and finished the job.

His breathing came in gasps, he shuddered and took her by the shoulders, freeing himself from her mouth but not before she knew the taste of him, a taste she'd want again and again.

She rested her cheek on his chest and he held her tight. She gave him little kisses, waiting for his breathing to return to normal.

"Why did you do that?" He asked, lifting her chin. "I want to pleasure you, not the other way around."

"You will, in more ways than one."

He kissed her forehead, her nose, her eyes, and then her mouth. "You're something special. You know that?"

"Yup. I do." She rolled off him. "If you can still walk, why don't you come to bed? I want to lie next to you."

"Good idea. This area is too small for me to do everything I want."

"Glad we're on the same page." She picked up the packages she'd brought home from the shop, and he followed her to bed.

This was going to be a good, good night. A memorable night that she could tuck away deep inside of her and pull out on cold, lonely nights.

They made love for hours, sampling different condoms and various positions, giggling like drunken fools as they did so. He seemed to want to keep it light as much as she did. Perhaps he was equally afraid that if he opened his heart there'd be no turning back.

CHAPTER TWENTY

Chase dropped Mila at work and returned to the falls. Devon had called while they were having their first sip of coffee to say that a helicopter would pick him up at ten sharp. He had it for one hour, and not to be late.

As if. Chase had a strange feeling about today. Like he was walking on a tight-wire and could tip the balance one way or another. Either he might make some great discovery or at any second disaster could strike.

Every nerve end in his body tingled and stood on high alert. This had only happened to him once before. The day his brother was killed in the motorcycle accident. He'd felt itchy all day, knowing something big was about to happen, not realizing the severity at the time.

His mother had left for the factory early, always getting up before dark, starting work at six in the morning. His brother had the two to midnight shift. Chase was finishing his last year of high school and working at the local Big Mac's after school. He never made it to work that night. At two in the afternoon he was pulled out of class. Told by the local cops that his brother had been in a bad accident and they'd take him to the hospital.

His mother had arrived before him. She was sitting in the ER waiting room, crying softly in a crumpled wet tissue. He'd found another one and handed it to her without a word, then took the seat next to her. She glanced at him with tired, red eyes.

"He quit today. Said he was going into the army and had already signed up. Guess he went drinking to celebrate," she said quietly. "Ya think he'll make it?"

"Don't know. What did the doctors say?"

"Haven't spoken to them yet, but those young cops, they said he ran smack dab into a post. Damn fool. Why'd he go and sign up with the army when we're at war, for Pete's sake. How could he do a dumb thing like that?" Her head bowed and he could see her shoulders shaking. "He'd have been killed overseas for sure. What does he know about fighting spooks in those jungles?"

He didn't bother to correct his mother, but put a hand on her arm for comfort. There was nothing to say, nothing to do but wait. Hours passed slowly, then a man in a white coat and a plastic cap came to speak with them.

"You Josh Carlton's family?" he asked.

They nodded.

"Is he…" Chase couldn't bring himself to ask.

"I'm sorry. He didn't make it. We did all that we could. The internal bleeding was too severe and he'd ruptured his lungs and liver." His eyes were sad as he spoke. "I'm very sorry."

His mother braced herself on a chair, and Chase gave her a worried look, afraid she'd collapse. "Well, that's that then," she said in a weary tone. "Thanks, doctor, for trying to save my boy."

"We have grief counselors if you'd like to speak with one," he said kindly.

"No, we'll be all right. Won't we, son?"

He nodded, too choked to speak. He'd never see his brother again. Never laugh with him, or make big grandiose plans that both of them knew would never work out. They hadn't always seen eye to eye, but he loved him just the same, faults and all. Worst thing was-- he'd never be able to tell him how proud he was for joining the army and wanting to get out.

Chase was seventeen, but was the man of the house now. Time to act like one.

"I'll take you home, Mom. And make all the funeral arrangements. Quit school. Get a job. Whatever it takes, Mom."

"You will do none of those things. You will graduate school and get out of here while the getting is good. That's what you will do for me, my son."

Six months later, he was gone.

Today was nothing like that day so many years ago. Today, the sun was shining, the world shivered with hope. His world was about to change again, and he had no idea how but embraced the notion. He'd come to Serendipity Falls for a reason, and if his instincts were correct, it'd be a good one.

While he waited he walked along the lake's edge, looking into the clear water as if he half expected to see a nugget of gold buried beneath the flat stones. It was that kind of day when miracles could happen to someone even as undeserving as himself.

He spotted a school of fish, some mossy boulders peeping out from a wide, sweeping overhead branch. A family of turtles sat on the shore next to the lake. Logs floated by, and then he heard a fluttering of wings and glanced up to see a hawk rise out of a tree and soar through the sky. Down shore, there were a couple of men in wading boots and lumber jackets fly fishing in the shallow water.

At precisely ten o'clock he heard the rotors of the chopper overhead, and saw the pilot nod to him as he indicated the pick up point. There was a ledge about fifty years away and Chase hurried toward it, keeping low and well away from the hovering craft and man eating blades.

As the helicopter hovered over the ledge, he climbed aboard and they rose quickly.

The pilot introduced himself as John Barnes, and asked where he'd like to go.

"Not sure exactly. Hoped you might help me out here."

"What did you have in mind?"

"Looking for something of interest. Seen anything unusual while you've been flying around here?" Chase shouted above the noise.

"Not much. Been flying these mountains for several years, and it's real pretty, but haven't seen anything out of the norm." He grinned. "Devon said you don't believe the myth of the love bug. That you're looking for something else to blame. You think it's an environmental issue, that right?"

"Not sure, but I'm checking out that possibility."

"Righteo, then. Hang on to your hat, and we'll scoot around and see what we can see."

Chase pointed to the falls. "Can you get me behind there?"

"I'll get as close as I can."

They circled the falls a few times but Chase couldn't see anything worth investigating. "Can you take me to the mines?"

"Well, son, we've got so many active mines around here, you'll need several days not hours. There's six gold prospecting maps and each one has hundreds of mines to choose from. They're tucked away in the mountains, the valleys, dry washes and deserts. So unless you've got all day and money to burn, got something specific?"

Chase rubbed his jaw. "Shit, man. I wish I did."

"Well, let's see. Riverside, San Bernardino and Kern, were all famous back in 1850. They're still active with prospectors and treasure hunters."

"Since our time is limited why don't you give me a general aerial view? Maybe something will jump out at me."

As requested, John showed him a few active mining sites, and pointed out dozens more. He might have to stay a month if he wanted to investigate each and every one for tainted waste, or suspicious activity. He didn't have a month. Or a week. Only a matter of days.

"Head back to the falls," he shouted, and the pilot circled back. The scenery was breath-taking and Chase hadn't wanted to admit to Devon, but he'd never been up in a helicopter before. It was a heady sensation and John was obviously an experienced pilot, who decided to give him a thrill ride.

He handed Chase some headphones, turned on some loud head banging music then dived down and raced along the shore. They skimmed just above the water, and caressed the mountain terrain, and the music pounded in his ears. He felt an adrenalin rush like no other.

They hovered over the falls for a few minutes and Chase could swear the mountain glittered. The harsh wet rocks seemed to glow, perhaps a reflection from the sunlight, or from the actual falls.

He pointed to the mountain above the falls. "Think we can get closer?" he shouted.

The pilot took off his head phones and zoomed over to where he was pointing. "What do you see?"

"Not sure, but my gut is churning knots right now. That's a good sign."

The clouds were wispy as they hung over the mountain, making visibility difficult at best and the flying risky, but Chase pushed on. "A little closer. I think I see something."

He glanced up at the sky and saw some writing like those marry me signs that pop up at football stadiums. First letter C….second letter U, third looked like a P, then an I. The next letter he couldn't make out, but it had an arrow pointing downward.

He blinked and rubbed his eyes. What did it spell? Was this a sign?

He glanced again trying to read the last letter but the writing disappeared, breaking up into white whiffs of clouds. "Did you see that?"

"See what?" John asked.

"Looked like writing and an arrow. Now it's gone."

"There's a lot of crazy shit going on around here, but an arrow? Dream on." John scoffed, "Leading us to something big—right?"

"Well, it does sound kind of stupid, but I was certain that I saw it." He rubbed his hands over his eyes. "No. Probably not. I have an active imagination."

CUPI – he thought about it for several minutes, but the only word that came to mind was Cupid. No! Couldn't be.

"Wait a sec." John squinted, and pushed the helicopter closer. "I don't think I've ever seen this before. Looks like a crater or something. See what I'm looking at?"

"I sure do. Is there a place you can put me down?"

"I'll have to circle back and drop you above. You'll have to make your own way down the side of the cliff. Could be extremely dangerous. I don't recommend it if you're not experienced with this kind of terrain, and especially without hiking equipment."

"I've done some hiking in my past, and I have a good feeling about this. Take me to a drop off area, and wait for me. I won't be long."

"You're one crazy dude, you know that?"

He nodded, and a few minutes later, John put the helicopter down and Chase climbed out. He went to the edge of the cliff and swore under his breath. He must be crazy to attempt this, but so had the early adventurers been crazy when they took off from Spain to find America. In comparison, this was Mickey Mouse stuff.

He gritted his teeth, and slid down a few feet, searching for a ledge and finding one. The crater was about forty feet below him and then he'd have to climb back up. No point wasting time. He slid a few more feet, and his boot dislodged some earth which crumbled away beneath him. He reached blindly for something to hang onto, and was clinging to the side of the mountain by his fingertips.

Sucking in a few quick breaths, he tried to analyze the situation and reach a possible conclusion. Hell. It was all bad. His dangling legs were twitching. Nerves that he didn't know existed began tingling in alarm. His fingers couldn't hold this much weight. He wasn't starring in some blockbuster movie. He was going to die and never know the secrets hidden behind the falls. Never see Mila again. Have children. Laugh in the sunshine. Cry in the rain. It was bad, bad, bad.

He gave himself a mental slap in the face. *Buck up, Bronco. If you're going to fall into the canyon a thousand feet below at least do it like a man. Not screaming, but fighting. Don't give up.*

A second later a rope dangled before his eyes. He blinked, wondering if like the letters, it would simply disappear.

"Loop this around yourself," John called down. "I've got it anchored to the chopper. It won't go anywhere."

"Are you crazy?" Chase yelled. It meant removing one hand to grab the rope and he wasn't at all sure that he could support his weight with only his left hand. Already his arms were being pulled out of their sockets, and two hands were better than one. Perspiration dripped from his brow, sliding down, down, down. His body would be next if he didn't act quickly.

Nothing ventured, nothing gained. It was a losing battle either way. He had to do it.

John yelled, "On the count of three."

Chase grabbed the rope on one. With shaking fingers, he put it around himself, and looped a knot. It was the best he could do.

"I've got you," John called down. He released some of the rope and Chase slithered down a few more feet. He stopped for a second to catch his breath and wipe sweat from his eyes then descended the rest of the way.

He got to the crater and sunk to the ground, panting with relief, mopping sweat from his brow. He'd made it this far. Getting back up would be another matter.

His legs felt like rubber when he got to his feet. He needed to have a good look around and get going. He'd only booked the chopper for an hour and the last thing he wanted was for John to leave him here.

He noticed a strange looking rock that wasn't a rock, but he didn't know what else to call it. Looked like a green fern-like stone that didn't belong. He had a gut feeling that this spiky object was directly involved with the crater. He noticed something stranger. Whatever had landed here had come down hard enough to split open a wedge in the side of the mountain.

He shoved the unusual looking piece in his pocket, and made his way to the narrow opening, wondering if an asteroid or meteorite had caused the crater. He looked inside the narrow wedge that might have been about a foot in width and twenty feet in length and his blood rushed fast and furious, pumping with excitement.

The mother lode.

Gold so bright he had to blink twice, winked back at him. And there it was. His story to tell. He'd find out what created the crater and cracked open the mountain and unearthed the gold.

It hadn't been an illusion. Gold did shine through the falls and probably sprinkled down into the lake below. The terrestrial object might have ejected some gas or something in the air, or it was the fine dust of gold sprinkles in the lake. This was the magic of Serendipity Falls.

CUPID

Oh, what a vain, useless cupid am I? What was I thinking writing my name in the cloud? Dear me, I may have given the secret away and I'm sworn by the oath that all cupids live by never to be revealed to humans. They may kick me out of the brotherhood and deservedly so. Crazy, foolish me! We have a convention each year to celebrate our triumphs and an award ceremony for the truly great cupids who have achieved the most success stories of the year. I have never won, but I thought I had a good chance this year since I cornered the market in Serendipity Falls. Not now, I'm afraid.

I can blame it on the altitude of course. I was very light headed and quite breathless flying over the falls. I mean, Mammoth has an elevation of ten thousand feet, and I wasn't that high, but I sure was way up there. I looked down at tree tops and saw birds eye to eye. Sweet, darling little things that looked quite confused to see me, I might add.

The moment I realized the enormity of my error I dispersed the letters as quickly as I could. Really, an arrow was all I needed, and that had worked rather brilliantly, I must say. Wasn't Chase excited to see the gold? Truthfully, so was I. I had no idea it was there, only that a meteorite had struck the mountain behind the falls, and I figured he could make something of that.

But, my, my, my. The gold glitters, and people will flock to see it. That young man might bring about the next gold rush and I'll have so much business that for sure I'll win Cupid of the Year! How could I not? Oh, it is grand, as long as the council doesn't hear wind of my faux pas, I will most likely be a shoo in.

I can't wait to see all the young people chasing their dreams of finding gold and everlasting love. My bow quivers in anticipation.

CHAPTER TWENTY-ONE

Chase waved to John and indicated he was ready to come up, and John helped haul him in. When he got back on solid ground, he knew he had to be careful what to report. The story couldn't break until he had all the details, and until he reported it personally on the nightly news.

"Anything down there?" John asked.

"Found this." He pulled the green rock from his pocket. "No idea what it is but I figured it was there for a reason. What do you think?"

"Don't know." John took it in his hand and tossed it around, looking at it from all angles. "Pretty. Looks interesting, that's for sure."

"Well, I'll have it checked out. Not sure what kind of story I'm going to get from it, but if a meteor hit behind the falls, maybe it left some debris that is causing this phenomenon around here. Either airborne or in the spring water."

"There you go. It's plausible, I must admit."

"Well, I don't have any evidence yet, so let's keep it to ourselves for now. When I know what it is, I'll release the story and you can be the hero of the piece."

"That's mighty fine of you."

"Well, without you saving my life down there, and you spotting this from the helicopter, there would be no story. I owe you."

"I'm happy that I could be of service."

"I'd buy you a drink to celebrate, but I guess you're still on duty."

"I am and I better get back, but must admit I enjoyed this little adventure."

"Likewise, although it did get a little hairy back on that ledge."

They climbed aboard the helicopter, strapped in, and then rose steadily away from the glittering falls. Chase looked back into the sky wondering if he'd see another message. He was sure it had been meant for him.

Being a self-proclaimed cynic, he didn't believe in cupids, but if by any wild chance there was one, he'd keep it a secret. The gold was enough to keep Serendipity humming for a great many years. He hoped Mila wouldn't be disappointed when he told her that Serendipity didn't have an angel, either.

The rest of the day was spent at the library, educating himself on meteorites and asteroids, then he scoured books on rocks and minerals. What he had in his hand appeared to be a moldavite – tektite thing, a molten terrestrial material ejected from a meteorite impact. He would have to get it authenticated of course, but that couldn't happen until tomorrow. He returned to Mila's home and wrote a rough draft for his story.

At six, Chase put his draft away, along with his green rock, and drove over to the mall to pick up Mila. "Hey, beautiful," he said with a kiss and a smile.

She kissed him back. "You look happy. Did you find something?"

"I did, and we're going to celebrate tonight. Dinner out. I'll tell you about it on the drive." He filled her in as best he could, giving details about his discovery, leaving out the part about the gold. He couldn't take any chances of the story leaking until he owned it.

"How will you get this thing, this tektite authenticated," she asked in a subdued voice.

"I'll take it to San Francisco tomorrow, and let rock experts have a look."

She nodded, but didn't say anything.

"It was an exciting day," he said, hoping for a little more enthusiasm. "Flying around the falls in a helicopter was crazy shit, man."

"I'm sure it was." She licked her lips and glanced straight ahead. Her entire body language was closed and guarded.

"I damn near fell off the side of the cliff trying to hike down to the crater," he said, hoping to loosen her up. "If John didn't have that rope handy, I'd have been a goner. No story. No dinner tonight. No great sex either."

"That was kind of stupid wasn't it? I mean going down a sheer mountain face without any gear? What were you thinking?"

He shrugged. "You know how important it is for me to get this story."

She rolled her eyes. "Enough to die for?"

"But I didn't. I'm fine, and the story is going to be dynamite."

"Glad you got what you wanted."

He parked in front of the restaurant and turned to look at her. "And you're not?"

"Sure I am. Now I can get rid of you."

She flounced off, and he followed her, shaking his head. So this is what was bothering her—well, they had both known all along that this was how it would end.

Mila slid into the nearest booth and picked up a menu. She didn't look up when he took the seat opposite.

He strummed the tabletop with his fingers, but she continued to ignore him. Her vibes were getting to him, making him darn right uncomfortable. What was it with women--they never knew from one day to the next what they wanted. She'd been telling him all along to get his story and get moving.

"You okay?" he asked softly. "I thought you'd be glad for me."

"I am." She gave him a quick look then glanced away, and he couldn't see her face because she had the menu right up to her nose.

The frizzy blonde-haired waitress named Sue came over to take their orders. "See you're still here," she said to Chase and gave him a wink. "I just love having you young couples come in here with that special glow about you."

"I have to leave tomorrow," he said, shooting a glance at Mila, "but then I'll be back to finish up my story."

Sue stood there, pen in hand. "I'm real sorry to hear that. Hope you come back to visit us," she shot a look at Mila, "real soon and often. Now what can I get you two for dinner? For our specials, we have a lovely pot roast or a prime rib dinner."

Chase glanced at Mila. "Prime rib for me. And we'll have a bottle of your finest wine, since we're celebrating."

"Celebrating, are you?" Her eyes twinkled. "Anything you'd like to share?"

"Yes. His leaving," Mila answered.

Sue's face flushed and she looked at her notepad. "Well, our wine selection isn't great but we have a decent Napa Pinot Noir or a Cabernet."

"Whichever is the most popular," he said with a friendly smile.

Mila sniffed. "I'll have the prime rib too. Medium rare, please," she told Sue.

"As rare as you've got," Chase said. "And a bowl of your Onion soup."

Mila wouldn't look at him, but she spoke to Sue. "Caesar salad, please."

When Sue left, Mila had no place left to look. She fiddled with her hands and seemed to find something interesting over his shoulder.

Finally he had enough. "Are you going to ignore me all night?"

"No...I..." she bit her lip and looked away.

"Mila, look at me. Please?"

She blinked rapidly, then lifted her head. "Okay. I'm acting like a jerk."

"No, you're not. You're being emotional and that's understandable. Neither of us know how to react."

"That's not true. We've been prepared for this, it's just…"

"I know. Prepared is one thing until it happens. I'm sorry."

"Don't be." She reached over and grabbed Chase's hands. "It's all right." She forced a smile, but he could see her eyes were burning bright. "You're leaving tomorrow. And I'm okay with that. Don't worry—we've had a wonderful few days together, and I for one won't regret a minute of it."

"Neither will I." He picked up one of her hands and gave it a kiss. "We can still be friends, maybe more. It's not like I live half way around the world."

"Not yet, but wait until you get your story out. Then networks everywhere will be clamoring for you. Chase Carlton reporting from Syria," she said in a gruff voice.

"Sure it's not as pretty as Serendipity Falls, but certainly will have plenty of action," he conceded.

When the wine arrived, Chase rehashed what he'd already told her, and reaffirmed that he'd be back by the end of the day.

She gave him a small smile that didn't reach her eyes. "I'm glad your work here is done. You must have been getting antsy."

"I wouldn't say that. Last night was something special. Every day is when I'm with you." He glanced away, uncomfortable with this conversation, but wanting to make things clear. "I'm going to miss you, you know."

"I'm going to miss you too, but I'm sure it'll only be temporary. Once we get back into our usual routine, things will be fine."

"I hope you're right." He squirmed in his seat, feeling like the biggest heel in the world. Making love to her the way he had, leaving her now…

"Yeah, well, if you find you can't live without me, you know where I am." She picked up her wine glass and took a big sip. "So what are your plans? I mean, after you write your story?"

"Not sure just yet." He took a hefty sip of wine too. "Let's forget business for a while and enjoy our meal. Okay?"

"Okay." She fiddled with the stem of her wineglass. "I think you should probably leave tonight. It might be best."

Chase nodded, but didn't reply. His stomach rumbled, and his throat closed so he had a hard time breathing. He glanced away and fought for control.

Sue brought them their soup and salad and they ate in silence. The easy friendship had shifted and Chase didn't know how to make it right.

* * *

Mila had no idea why she'd blurted that out, but once the words were said, she couldn't take them back. It was better for him to leave. The longer he stayed the more she would want him too. And the deeper the wound when he left. She'd known heartache and she didn't like it. That awful feeling as though your heart had been ripped right out of you, the sleepless nights, and bone weary days. The crying jags, the numbness that invaded your soul and felt like it would never leave. She hated it all, and refused to let it happen again.

She played with her dinner, eating a small portion of the beef and potatoes, but Chase devoured his like it was his last supper. Obviously the idea of leaving didn't bother his appetite at all.

Men. Heartless creatures.

Well, she wouldn't let it ruin her dinner either. She took another swallow of wine, and speared an asparagus. She picked it up with her fork and waved it in his direction. "I'll drive you to the airport."

The Mammoth county airport was only a twenty-minute drive, but of course, they probably wouldn't have flights out this evening. That wouldn't work. She should just apologize and ask him to stay the night. That's what a civilized person would do.

But not a civilized person trying desperately to avoid a broken heart.

"You don't have to do that. I can catch a cab."

"A cab? Forget it. It'll cost an arm and a leg, and there won't be any flights out until morning. I didn't think of that when I offered."

"That's fine. You've already done so much for me."

He resumed eating, and savagely she bit into her asparagus and swallowed it whole, wishing it was a part of his anatomy she'd devoured. Just, "that's fine—you've done so much for me?" Really?

"Whatever." She sat up straight, fighting a terrible urge to say something she might regret.

"Look." Chase reached out to touch her hand and she flinched, and pulled hers away. "I don't have to leave until tomorrow, and I had planned to return. You're the one pushing me out."

She wondered what he'd do if she picked up the bottle of wine and poured it over his annoying head. Didn't he realize how obnoxious he sounded? Not caring one way or the other if he stayed with her another night, if he slept with her or not, well, that was just plain insulting.

She had a good mind to...to...cry.

She pushed her wineglass aside. "If you're finished, perhaps we could leave. I know you want to get going, and I have some important details to work out for Devon and Tara's wedding."

"I'll get the bill." Without waiting for the waitress, he slid out of the booth and marched up to Sue, taking money out of his wallet.

She watched him walk away and felt his loss with only a few steps. He was leaving her tonight. The thought stilled her heart, but she lifted her chin high, stood up and walked to the door. Turning, Mila waved goodbye to Sue, but couldn't speak to the woman, whose worried expression replaced her usual pleasant and smiling face.

She had to leave, get home, and be alone before she broke down and cried in front of him and Sue, and all the other diners, mostly locals she barely knew.

What if he packed his bags and called a cab? Would she let him go or ask him to stay? No. That wouldn't happen. Not tonight, not tomorrow, not in this lifetime. Whether she wanted him or not, loved him or not.

Damn love bug, or Venus, or whoever the hell put the two them together. Why couldn't they have left her and Chase alone? They'd been happy. Not deliriously so, but certainly content. And who wanted to walk around being delirious all the time? Surely it was over-rated.

Just then, she felt a sting above her right breast. She rubbed it absently.

What was she going to do? Serendipity Falls didn't have an overly large population of available men. But maybe with the influx of new people flocking here, some wonderful guy might come along in a few years and save her from her maiden voyage. She didn't want to live and die an old maid.

And, truth be known, she didn't really have anyone interesting to call up and invite over for sex. The large vibrator got a good workout once in a while, and that was about it. Fondly, she called it George.

Well, she and George would have to keep company for a while, because Chase had big plans and was moving on out. He had important things to do, like deliver the up-to-date news around the troubled spots in the world. It sounded exciting. More interesting than hanging around Serendipity, watching and waiting for something remarkable to happen. The most remarkable thing in her lifetime had been the excitement over the love bug, and watching people fall passionately in love. The second most remarkable thing had been the moment Chase had appeared. Or was it the over way around? Had he been the most remarkable thing to happen in her lifetime?

Possibly, yes. Probably. Absolutely! But what difference did it make now? He had to go, she had to stay and that was all there was to it. She needed to buck up, put her big girl panties on, wave goodbye, and watch him disappear forever.

CHAPTER TWENTY-TWO

Chase didn't know what to say to Mila to make things right. What could a guy say to a girl when he was ready to leave? He had feelings too. They'd both been hit by this Serendipity fever and he loved Mila, whether he'd wanted to or not. He *loved* her. But he needed to see if it would last once he got away, back to his own life.

In San Francisco, in his own apartment, his space, he'd be able to evaluate his feelings better. Were they real or simply a manifestation from something in the air? The gold that filtered into the water, the meteorite that perhaps emitted a gas—or Cupid himself? He had no firm conclusion to the story he'd eventually write, no scientific proof, only a few theories to offer and let the readers make their own assumption.

The fact was, as difficult as it was to admit as a reporter, that Serendipity Falls was a happy place and he didn't really know why. The itty bitty gold dust in the water? The lucky green tektite? There was no definitive answer.

That would be his report, making his job in Serendipity as a journalist obsolete. He and Mila had agreed he would leave to pursue his life-long dream as soon as he'd discovered the magic of Serendipity Falls.

Mila drove them back to her place, and he could tell from the sadness in her eyes and her rigid body language that she was hurting inside. He wanted to wrap her up in his arms and kiss away every misgiving, every fear, every tear, and tell her that everything would be all right. But he didn't know if it would. Until he left, he had no answers for either of them.

Could they survive without each other? Would their longing disappear or haunt them day and night? Right now, the idea of being without her was tearing him in two.

Silently, she opened the door and followed him in. She went to her bedroom while he quickly gathered his belongings and packed them in his duffle bag. He picked up the guitar he'd had no inclination to play, and sat down to wait for Mila to come out of her room.

He wouldn't leave without a proper goodbye.

Strumming the guitar, his fingertips found the right chords, and without conscious effort a beautiful melody drifted out. He didn't know the music, it just came from somewhere deep inside.

Mila walked in, tears in her eyes. "What is that?"

"I don't know. I'm not thinking, just playing." Would she kiss him? Beg him to stay? He wanted her so badly, but pride kept him still.

"It's beautiful." She sniffed and took a tentative step in his direction.

"I'll call it Ode to Mila," he said with a rueful smile. His heart was heavy but he didn't want to burden her any more than he already had. Light, he needed to keep things light. "Come sit with me for a minute."

She threw her arms around his neck, kissing him and crying at the same time. "Oh, Chase. I'm going to miss you so much."

"I know, sweetheart. I'm going to miss you too." He held her close, breathing in her scent. As if it were the last time. But he knew about last times, didn't he? His father had walked away and never returned—then his brother. They'd had breakfast that last morning, then by the afternoon he was gone. Just like that.

"I want only the best for you," she said. "You know that." Her eyes lifted to meet his and she stroked his face. "Go. Make your news. Become all that you want to be. Make me proud."

His throat was raw, and his eyes burned. There was a painful fist around his heart, squeezing, and the agony was real. Gawd, how we wanted to be weak and sweep her into his arms and make love to her one last time.

But, for both their sakes, he needed to be strong.

He kissed her softly, tenderly, then gently removed her hands from around his neck. He couldn't feel her sweet breasts against his chest any longer, or the brush of her cheek, the softness of her lips, the enticing taste, smell, warmth and feel of her, this enchanting, beautiful woman he loved. Mila.

His heart lurched. He felt a pull, a need so strong that it was a physical ache, perhaps like a druggie needing a fix. She intoxicated him. She was more than a high, she was the life blood needed to survive.

And that scared the shit out of him.

He stood up, fighting every urge in his body to pick her up, take her to bed, and to stay safe and never leave. But what kind of a man would that make him? A coward unwilling to face the unknown, the danger, the very things he'd always wanted. Alone. Without Mila. This madness took over in less than a week. He could stay away for that long, to prove the fever of Serendipity was curable with time and distance. A week, to prove to himself that he was in charge of his own destiny. No love bug, no angels. No Cupid.

"I need to go."

"I know. It's all right." She stepped back, folding her arms over her waist and sniffing back a tear. "I'll call you a cab. You understand that I can't wait here with you until it comes."

She kissed him softly, then walked into the bedroom and closed the door.

His rubbed the ache over his broken heart.

* * *

She didn't cry. Not until she heard the cab pull up to the house, and the sound of the door close behind him - then she released the silent tears that her heart had cried. Her former love paled in comparison to what she felt for Chase – in both instances she'd dared to love despite the risk. Was she stupid? Insane?

By morning, she had an empty box of tissues next to her. Her eyes were so swollen she could hardly see the light of dawn creep over the mountains. Good news was, she was all cried out. There wasn't a tear left in her, and good riddance, she thought.

Today was a brand new day. Chase was gone and she could get back to normal. Concentrate on what was important. Her business—a shop filled with everything a bride needed to make her dream wedding come true. How ironic that seemed, selling romance, planning weddings, especially now that her heart was breaking. Here in Serendipity, happiness abounded; it surrounded her on a daily basis, in people's smiles, in their glances, and in their hearts.

She'd always been immune to it, until now. She should be grateful to Chase for opening her up inside and allowing her to see what she'd been missing. Instead of gratitude, she only felt pain.

Prickles of tears floated behind her eyelids but being the brave soldier that she was, she fought them back. *No more. Be gone, worthless tears.* She could do this. Survive and thrive. One day at a time.

After she'd showered and dressed, and iced her eyes to help with the swelling, she layered on the makeup to camouflage the red rimmed lids. She needed her happy face on to meet and greet the exuberant couples coming through her doors. Her clients deserved nothing less.

From the moment she opened there seemed to be a never ending parade of giggly brides-to-be. Busloads of new arrivals bursting with excitement had picked this very day to waltz through her store.

Mila, being the consummate actress and practical business woman, took it all in stride, offering chilled glasses of champagne to her customers, enticing them with lovely aphrodisiacs, smiling, smiling, smiling, while hiding her broken heart.

Tara came in late in the afternoon, just before Mila was ready to close. She'd come to try on the wedding dress Mila had selected, but after one look at her, she pulled her into a fierce hug.

"What happened? You didn't push him away, did you?"

When Mila shook her head and sniffed back tears, Tara gentled her voice, and poured them both a full glass of champagne. "Come sit. Tell me everything. Where is that delicious man, Chase?"

Mila, knowing Tara would understand, told her sister of the heart everything – including how she had to let him go. For his own good.

"I understand, hon, but he said he'd be back, didn't he?"

"Yes," Mila nodded. "I told him it wasn't a good idea for him to see me. We need a clean break."

"Perhaps you do," Tara surprised Mila by saying. "You both need to see that your love is real and a little distance can do that. He needs to go back to his life to discover what's true and what's not."

Mila hiccupped. "That's pretty much what he said. This seems really real to me."

"Because it is!" Tara handed Mila another tissue. "So until that time, you can't sit around and mope. We have my wedding to plan. And you need a date. I'm going to call my contractor. You remember, Ty. Handsome, charming."

Chilled, Mila sat back in surprise. "Of course I remember him, but I'm really not ready to date anyone."

Tara waved away her response. "Fine. It won't be a date. But he can escort you to my wedding, can't he?" Tara gave her a hug. "You said it yourself, you'll need someone to dance with, and someone who can make you laugh."

"I laughed with Chase. And I don't feel much like laughing anymore." Had she been wrong, not using her feminine wiles to trap him with her for eternity? No. It had been the right thing to do, even if it hurt.

"And if Chase shows up, all the better. An extra man at a wedding is always a good thing."

"He won't. He's made it very clear that Serendipity is the last place he wants to be. Invite Ty if you want - I promise I won't do anything to mar your perfect day."

"Oh, sweetie, I wasn't thinking about that. Only you, and how unhappy you must be right now."

"I'll live. Hang on a sec." Done with the depressing stuff, Mila dashed off, and came back with Tara's wedding gown. "Now go. Try this on. I can't wait to see you in it."

"Wow. It's gorgeous." Tara held it up, admiring the dress. "I'll slip it on, although I can see it's going to be perfect."

Mila refilled her champagne glass, noticing that Tara hadn't touched hers. Tara changed in the dressing room while Mila waited impatiently. Would it fit? Would it be the right style? When she came out, Mila gasped, and nearly dropped her glass. "Tara! Did you see yourself? You look absolutely stunning. Do you like it?"

The strapless gown had mother-of-pearl beads on the bodice and then fell straight down, clinging to her petite figure as if custom designed. The simplicity and elegance suited Tara to a T. Mila felt a thrill of pride that she'd discovered the dress, that she, the owner of Wedding Fever, had helped another bride make their day perfect.

"I love it!" Tara twirled, and posed in front of the floor length mirror. "It's gorgeous. How can I ever thank you?"

"You just did, and you're going to be the prettiest bride Serendipity has ever seen."

She grinned with delight. "Mila, hon. I'm also going to need undergarments and a sexy negligee for the wedding night. Can you help me select a few things, and just add that to my tab?"

"I'd be happy too. But there is no tab. This is my personal present to you." She tilted her champagne glass in Tara's direction. "A gift for marrying my brother and making him the happiest man I know." A dagger-like pain sliced her heart, as she realized that Chase couldn't have been happy, or he'd have found a reason to stay.

"Mila, I'm so lucky to have not only Devon, but you, the sister I never had."

For the first time that day, Mila's spirits picked up, and her smile was warm and genuine. "Me too. I always longed for a sister. I can't wait to be an aunt."

Tara put a hand over her mouth, and her eyes sparkled. "Can I tell you a secret?"

"You're pregnant?" Mila guessed. "Oh, I hope that's it." At Tara's nod, she clapped her hands. "Does Dev know?"

"Not yet. I only found out a few hours ago. I'm going to tell him tonight."

"In that case you need to take a little something extra home." She eyed some sexy lingerie and a beautiful satin robe, and slipped them into a pink Wedding Fever bag. "Wear this when you give him the exciting news."

"I will, Mila. And you'll have to be a Godmother too."

"Matron of honor and Godmother," she answered, her insides warm and fuzzy. "How wonderful is that? I'm so thrilled for the both of you."

And it never would have happened without the mysterious forces at work.

CHAPTER TWENTY-THREE

Chase contacted a few notable rock and gem specialists in San Francisco, confirming his find. The third shop, From Junk to Gem, had a retired Geology professor on staff.

"Where'd you say you got this?" An old man sat at a desk full of rock fragments. The placard read Professor Brown, Geologist.

"Mammoth County," Chase answered.

"Hard ta believe," the professor said, eyes on the stone. He darted a quick glance at Chase. "You see, moldavites are exclusive to the Czech Republic. Now, tektites are located in four locations around the world, but not these green gemstones. That's a fact."

"I know what I found," Chase said. "And where I found it. Right behind Mammoth Falls in California."

The old man shook his head, turning the stone around, scrutinizing it from every angle. "Only documented find of tektites in North America was Chesapeake Bay – Maryland, and that was not a moldavite. Not to say you're pulling a fast one, kid, but this can't be." He pushed his glasses up the ridge of his nose. "It's perplexing, that's for sure."

The owner of the shop picked up a piece of moldavite that he'd had in stock and compared it to the much larger, colorful piece Chase brought in. "It's the same. How could one show up in California?"

"That's a good question, one I'm hoping to answer," Chase replied. Wanting to appear a little knowledgeable about his find, he added, "I read up on them before coming here. I know they're condensed rock vapors formed after a meteorite impact." He shrugged. "Found this in a crater behind the falls."

"Well, I'll be damned," the old fellow said.

"I'm doing an article for WUX News. Need someone to verify this piece of rock and the crater site. The station will pick up the tab."

"I can recommend a name or two." The professor picked up the stone again, almost in awe. "This is a beauty. Bigger than most. We could polish it up and it would be worth something."

"It's not for sale," Chase said firmly.

Determined to get answers, Chase decided to brave the old man's derision and asked, "Is there any way that the vapors or the moldavites could release a gas or energy in the air, causing a surge of well-being, or, specifically, er...love?"

The professor's bushy brows shot up and he grinned, showing a few missing back teeth. "What kind of story are you writing?"

Straightening his shoulders, Chase tapped the table full of rocks. "There has been a documented surge of weddings around this town, and I'm thinking it has something to do with the meteor landing."

The professor laughed himself into a coughing fit. "Pure science fiction is what you're writing, son."

"Not necessarily. I did my research and discovered that in ancient times moldavites were thought to be a mystical stone that could bring good luck and fulfill your wishes." He shrugged. "I'm just saying. Perhaps it could happen." Chase didn't know the truth from squat, but he knew he could slant this story anyway he liked. People loved love.

Professor Brown wiped the smile from his face. "It's not impossible, I suppose."

Chase wrote down the contact numbers of the experts he recommended, then left the store with a new spring in his step. A few days later, he returned to Serendipity Falls with his film crew and a team of experts. They'd confirmed that yes, a meteorite had impacted the area behind the falls, and estimated it had occurred four years ago but were unclear as to why it had gone undetected.

"Four years ago," Chase told Mike, pretty pleased with the results.

"Coincides perfectly with the wedding boom," the cameraman said.

Combining poetic prose with scientific terminology, he sat down and wrote his piece, proclaiming that the meteorite strike had created a crater and opened a crack in the side of the mountain. Gold had filtered down into the falls, possibly causing a release of energy into the air or a chemical in the spring water. Smaller pieces of moldavites were uncovered and if they actually did possess powers to bring luck and the fulfillment of wishes as earlier believed, then this could also be an important factor to the wedding fever in this small town. He concluded his report by stating that the falls shimmered with gold and made Serendipity a national treasure, a sight-seeing destination as worthy as Mount Rushmore.

He milked it for all it was worth and the people bought it.

At home, alone, he relished the news media picking up on this story but wasn't at all sure if he did Serendipity more harm than good. Money hungry people were flocking to the area, once again lured by the promise of gold.

In the past ten days he'd been back and forth to the falls but hadn't seen Mila. At first he avoided her, not wanting to cause her anymore heartache or distress, but with all the activity surrounding the site, he wouldn't have had the time for a personal visit. Just as well. If she felt anything like he did, she was suffering enough already.

Had he lost a limb, the ache couldn't have been worse. It was real and it was strong, with him every minute of the day. Determined to get rid of it, he made a point of going out most nights, having drinks with friends, flirting with pretty girls. Nothing worked. Pretty girls were just pretty girls—they weren't Mila, with the sparkling eyes.

Right when his career had reached a new high and his self esteem had peaked, he was at his most miserable. He'd always loved his home on the beach, small and quiet as it may be, but now the loneliness made it seem empty and barren. Even the call of the surf didn't have any allure. He ached for Mila. Did she feel the same?

Well, there was only one way to find out. He needed to see her again, to be certain that she was fine, getting along well without him. One more trip to Serendipity would ease his mind. She'd bounced into his life, his heart, and even if she was over him and his love one-sided, he'd never regret a second of their time together.

Due to his new celebrity status at the news station he didn't hesitate to request a few days off, saying he had some unfinished business in Serendipity Falls. Cameraman Mike had let the cat out of the bag, telling everyone that Chase had caught the love bug himself. He received a lot of teasing and a few pats on the back when he announced he was going back for a short visit.

He drove straight to the mall but found the wedding shop closed. It was Saturday, and the sign on the door said it would reopen Monday. Was she sick? She never took more than a day off. Worried now, he strode over to the coffee shop across from her store and ordered an espresso, hoping for a little conversation to go with the double shot of adrenalin.

"You new here?" the attractive barista asked, giving him a flirtatious smile.

"I've been around for the past few weeks." He offered his hand. "Chase Carlton from WUX News. I'm doing a story about the wedding fever going on, and came to ask the woman from the shop over there a few questions. You wouldn't know where she is, by any chance?" He gave her the full benefit of his dimpled smile.

She beamed back at him. "Mila. Sure. She's at a wedding. Her brother's getting married today."

"Really? Would you know where?"

"No, not sure that I do. But he and his brother run a bar in Mammoth. The Cock and Bull. Right in the town center. Ask anyone. They can tell you where it is."

"Thanks so much." He tossed her a ten. "Keep the change."

"Come back and see me sometime."

"I'm sure to see you around." He winked and walked out, sipping on his espresso.

It took him twenty minutes to drive up the hill and he arrived before noon. Luckily the bar was open, although mostly empty. Two lumberjack types were playing a game of pool. No one else was in sight.

He took a stool at the bar and after a few minutes the younger brother Kyle appeared through a swinging door.

"I'll be with you in a sec," he called, then went back carting in boxes of liquor.

"Need some help?" Chase asked.

Kyle looked up and recognized him. "Oh, it's you. What are you doing back in town? Don't you have some other nightly news to report?"

"I came to see Mila and figured you might know where she is. Today's the wedding, right?"

Kyle ignored the question and answered instead, "I don't keep tabs on her, but even if I did, don't see why her whereabouts should concern you."

"What's that supposed to mean?"

"Well, you took off didn't you? Never called her again. Too busy being the big shot, right?"

"I was just doing my job." He gave Kyle a self-deprecating grin. "If you saw it, you'd know the news story was a healthy blend of fact and fiction, with some speculation on my part."

"Shit. You know what you did here, right? Crazy folks are coming in by the boatloads, camping out near the falls. Everybody wants a piece of that gold." He ran a hand through his unruly hair. "Wish you'd never gone near the place. The locals liked things fine the way they were. The love bug myth didn't hurt anybody. It brought joy and happiness to a lot of people. This is going to bring crime and corruption. Nothing good will come of it."

"I hope you're wrong, but I'm concerned too. I've had meetings with environmentalists, the governor, anyone who'd listen, suggesting that they declare this a national park, or wall it off, so no one can get near the gold. It's too dangerous."

"Well, until that happens, people will be foolish enough to try. Danger never kept anyone away from the chance to amass a fortune."

"I agree with you, and I'm lobbying to keep this a protected area. If they open this area up for excavation, it could be deadly."

"Why don't you go on TV and tell the damn people that? Maybe they'd just turn around and go home."

Chase swore. "The news station has never had better ratings. A 21st Century gold rush, they're calling it. They don't care about the risk or possible damage. This is a big win for them."

"Right. And you're the asshole who shouted it out to the world."

"I had no choice, and even if I did, I'd still have done the same. I'm a journalist and that's what we do. Good or bad, people should be informed."

"So what's going to happen if they don't protect the area? People are going to die, man." Kyle shook his head. "I hope like hell that you have some influence because we're going to need it."

"I hear you, and trust me I'll do what I can." He sucked in a breath and released it slowly. "The gold needs to stay where it is. If people come along and try to remove it, they might destroy the very thing that makes Serendipity Falls so special."

"Fine. We both want to save Serendipity from speculators. But how are we going to do that?"

"I don't know. Wish I did." Chase rubbed his jaw. "I'd love to discuss this some more, but I'm really here to see Mila."

"She's probably with Tara. Everyone's busy getting ready." Kyle went back to work. "I doubt if she'll want to see you anyway. She's going to the wedding with Ty. He's the contractor Tara hired to fix up the B&B joint she bought."

"Who the hell is Ty? She didn't mention him to me."

He shrugged. "They've been out a few times this week."

"Shit." Chase put his hands on the bar and leaned in. "I've got to get to that wedding."

The door opened and Devon strode through. He stopped when he saw Chase. "What are you doing here?"

"I just explained all that to Kyle. I'm here to see Mila." He lifted his chin, meeting his gaze man to man. "This is between us, and I'm not leaving until I've had a word with her."

"Well, she doesn't want to see you."

"I need to hear that from her own mouth."

"Then you will." He jerked his head. "She's standing right behind you."

Chase turned slowly and there she was. His jaw dropped. His heart speeded up, and the ache inside of him nearly dropped him to his knees.

"Mila." His voice was unsteady and he felt heat creep up his neck. "How have you been?"

"I'm fine, but you'd have known that if you called."

Oh, boy. She was gonna give it to him good. Well, he could take that, he could take anything as long as she kept talking and didn't walk away.

He reached out a hand but she evaded it, and slid onto a stool leaving space between them. Space that he longed to close.

"You did a good job with the news report," she said, with a who-gives-a-shit shrug. "Not bad, considering."

"Considering what?"

"Considering you don't know a damn thing more than you did a month ago. It's still hocus pocus. A mystery that'll never be solved."

"Okay. What if I told you that I think its Cupid?"

She laughed. "Then I'd think you're more of a moron than you already are."

"Okay. It's Venus, the Goddess of Love. Happy?"

"I'm happy. Delightfully so. Dev's getting married, and I'm the matron of honor. Why wouldn't I be happy?"

Devon and Kyle were both listening and it was difficult for Chase to tell her how much he'd missed her and wanted her, with the two of them hearing every word.

"I hoped you might miss me."

"Oh, so you wanted me to be unhappy?"

"I didn't say that." He grimaced. "I was miserable, and just wanted to know if you were too."

"No, I'm not miserable. There. Now you know. If that's all, you can leave. I'm sure Syria is waiting for you. Matter-of-fact, I think I hear her calling."

"You're a piece of work." He jumped off his seat, and before she could react he was kissing her. "There. That's one way to shut you up."

"You're a jerk, you know that?"

"I know plenty of things and one of them is you shouldn't be going out with Ty tonight." He tried to control the flash of anger and jealousy, but it was a losing battle. He exhaled loudly. "Who the hell is he, anyway?"

"He's wonderful. Handsome. Owns a successful construction company. Great skier. Likes fine wine."

"I hate him already." He looked into her eyes, hoping desperately to see some forgiveness there. "So why don't you ditch him and take me?"

"I can't do that. He's been invited by Tara, and I'm seated right next to him." Her lips curved into a smug smile. "Perhaps you could ask Devon if you could do a news piece on their wedding."

Chase glanced at Devon, the bunched up muscles in his shoulders tight. "Any chance?"

"No fucking way."

"Well, there you have it," Mila said sweetly. "No fucking way."

Kyle snorted. "Sorry, Chase. Want a beer before you leave?"

"No, thanks." He shrugged, and gave one last look at Mila.

"Have a great wedding Devon, and I wish you and Tara ever-lasting happiness."

"Thanks, man," Devon grumbled and offered his hand.

Chase shook it, then he clapped him on the shoulder. "Where're you getting married? Big city hotel?"

"Nope. Right here at the Cascade Resort, where Tara works."

"Well, have a good one." He winked at Mila, then whistling like a man without a care in the world, he waltzed out the door.

He knew the location for the wedding and he'd see them all there.

CHAPTER TWENTY-FOUR

Chase had all afternoon to kill, so he drove down to the Serendipity mall and found himself a dark suit, a white shirt, flashy pink tie, and dress shoes for his evening attire. If he got tossed out on his head, at least he'd look good on his way through the door. He got a trim and a shave, hoping to give this Ty guy a run for his money.

No matter what Mila had told him, he knew the truth.

She was in love with him, every bit as much as he loved her. The proof was in the kiss. He'd felt the simmering heat between them, heard her soft sigh, and if the two big brothers hadn't been watching his every move, he'd have taken it further and broken down every last ounce of resistance.

Tucking his new purchases into the trunk of his BMW, he left the mall, needing to find a room for the night. He called the first place that came to mind, the Grand Cascade resort, and they had one room available—a suite. He booked it.

An hour later he was hanging out in his lavish suite, checking out the huge spa bath, the king sized bed, the inviting bath robes, the fully stocked mini bar, and wondered what Mila was doing right now, this very minute. She would love this room, and might even get all worked up like she had the night her Rover had the dead battery. God, he hoped so. There was nothing reserved about this woman—she was the most passionate female he'd ever met. And the only one he wanted.

He still had a job to do in San Francisco, and she had hers here, but because they were in love they would figure it out. He no longer wanted or needed an overseas post. That had been a youthful dream from a young man who thought he had to set the world on fire to prove himself. Now, all he cared about was Mila. He wanted to be with her forever, and protect the way of life in Serendipity Falls.

His future was up in the air, but he'd figure it out eventually. He could open a newspaper or become the town mayor. Better yet, he'd head up an environmental group that would protect the area behind the falls. This was his discovery and now it would be his legacy to leave it as intact as he'd first found it.

Chase went to the windows and drew the drapes back to relish the view. The twilight sky, with pink and mauve hues highlighted the spectacular mountain which spread before him. The mountains were a part of him now, and after all his roaming and trying to find a place for himself, this home had found him. He took a small velvet package out of his overnight bag and put it on the counter. He'd had Junk to Gems design a pendant and a ring designed with a piece of the moldavite. The beautiful green gem surrounded by diamonds was set in gold filigree. His gift to Mila.

He patted the velvet bag and smiled, imagining her face and surprise. If the ancient belief about moldavites

held truth, then good luck and the fulfillment of his wishes would come later tonight.

He called down for a bottle of champagne to be delivered to the room at precisely eleven o'clock, then took a long hot shower.

* * *

Mila spent the entire afternoon in a daze. She hadn't expected Chase to appear. Not today. Not ever. Although her stomach jumped and her pulse raced like a thoroughbred, she had to keep calm and not act like a love crazy fool. This was Tara's night. Not hers.

Had it really been yesterday when she'd considered the idea of sleeping with Ty? They'd been out three times, it was a romantic night and they were both guests of the hotel. She knew he expected her to, and she'd thought, maybe it was time. Not that she had any stirrings that way, but she'd hoped it might help ease her heartache over Chase. Make her want him less. She'd tried to convince herself that a man like Ty could erase those memories and begin new ones, but one glance at Chase had made it all clear. He was the only man for her. Now and forever.

Although Chase had fooled her brothers, Mila knew he wasn't giving up. She had felt it in the kiss. She'd known instinctively that his feelings ran deep. His sweet mouth had captured hers in an honest, bone melting kiss that had stolen her breath and reclaimed her heart.

Where was he, she wondered? If she knew him as well as she thought she did, he'd be somewhere in this hotel. Would he show up at the wedding, and what would she do if he did?

She eyed herself in the mirror, seeing herself as Chase would. Her dark hair waved around her shoulders and her make-up was artfully applied to showcase her large, luminous eyes. Her cheeks were rosy and her face glowed. Mila slipped on her pale blue evening gown and hurried to Tara's suite to help her dress.

Tara opened the door at her light knock. "You're early. I'm glad. Cindy's here and we're having a glass of champagne to help us relax." Cindy was Tara's closest friend in the village and worked with her at the hotel as an assistant pastry chef. She was the single bridesmaid, and although not wearing a matching dress to Mila's it was also in a soft blue.

"Good idea." She pulled herself a small glass and then turned to admire her sister-in-law. "You look so beautiful. Here, let me just straighten the hem a little."

Nothing really needed to be done, the dress fit her figure perfectly, and fell seamlessly to the floor. It didn't have a million tiny little buttons like so many others, it was simply elegant. Like her new sis.

"So, where is Sheila? Did you invite her to join us?" Sheila was Tara's father's new wife, and they had only recently met.

"No, but we both had our hair and nails done together. I figured that was enough girl time," Tara answered with a smile, then took a sip of champagne. "I wanted a moment alone with my two best friends."

"You nervous?"

"Not in the least." She laughed. "Suppose I should be, but hey. How can anything go wrong when I already know I have a hundred percent chance of happiness?"

Cindy grinned. "Just because marriages last forever here doesn't guarantee happiness, does it?"

"Sure it does." Tara took Cindy's hand. "Speaking of which, how are things with you and Ken?"

"Moving along. Not like the whirlwind of yours, but at a nice pace. A normal pace," she added with emphasis.

Tara spun to Mila. "What about you? Things heating up with Ty?"

"Uh—not sure." Mila pressed her hand to her stomach as if that would stop the nervous twists and turns. "Guess who came by the Cock and Bull today looking for me?" She didn't wait for the girls to answer. "Chase!"

"How do you feel about that?" Cindy asked.

"You still love him…" Tara said.

"My heart went into overdrive. I'm not sure if we can work things out, or even if he's here to stay. We didn't get a chance to talk without Kyle and Devon."

"I can imagine," Tara said with a sympathetic nod. "Protective big brothers. Well, you'll know one or the other soon enough."

"I guess so." Mila decided now was a good time to escape. "Well, girls, I'd love to stay and chat, but I really want to see Mom and Dad for a few minutes. I'll catch up with you later," she said to Cindy, and hugged Tara. "You are the most gorgeous bride I've ever seen, and that's quite a few," she said with a grin.

Mila let herself out, then dashed downstairs to find her parents. They'd only arrived two days ago and she had barely seen them. She found them in the lounge.

"How are the groom's parents holding up?" she asked, giving them both a warm hug and kiss. "Drinking martinis I see. Not a bad idea."

"You want one, Mila?" her father asked.

"No, better not. Maybe a teensy glass of chardonnay." She took her mother's hand and held it up, admiring her dress. "Great outfit, Mom. You look beautiful as always."

Catherine O'Reilley wore a lemon colored suit that showed her petite figure to perfection, and brought out the warm sparkle of her blue eyes. Her mother was ravishing, and her father, Donald, at sixty, was a fine looking man. Tall and slim with receding gray hair, he looked fit and healthy, and still very much in love with his wife.

The wedding was less than an hour away, but spending some private time with her parents was priceless. She'd missed them so much after they'd moved to Hawaii, and with her business in such demand, their visits together were few.

"So, have you been seeing this young man, Ty Jamison, very long?" her mother asked. "We both liked him, didn't we, Donald?"

"Yes, a hard worker. Seems like he has a good business up here. Told me that he's under contract with several hotels, with more bids pouring in. He's actually turning down jobs." Her father nodded at her, as if putting in his vote for the win.

Ty had joined them the previous evening for the rehearsal dinner, dazzling her parents and both brothers too. "Yes, he's very busy, just as I am. We haven't known each other long. Only a few weeks." She wished that Chase had the chance to prove himself – but he'd opted out of the game. Unless her instincts were right, and he showed up at the wedding. Then, who knew?

"Well, he certainly seems to have his eye on you." Her mother laughed. "Couldn't keep those baby blues off you last night." She patted Mila's hand. "Oh, I do want you to find someone special and he might be the one! Now, with Devon almost married, I'm hoping you'll be next. All this work you do. It's no life for a woman. You need a husband and children of your own."

"Mom." She drew out the word and rolled her eyes. "Really? What century is this?"

Her father chuckled. "Now, now, Cathy, darling, you know that young women don't need a man to be happy. They have gay friends to go out with, and what-have-you. Things have changed."

"And George. Can't forget George," Mila said crisply. Gay friends? What were they watching on television? Modern Family?

"Who's George?" her dad asked. "Another fellow after you?"

"No. It's not important." She took a big sip from her wine, giving a thumbs up to the bartender. "I've gotta go in a minute but I just wanted to say how much I love you, and miss you, and wish we had more time to spend together. Can't you stay a few weeks? Do you have to get back to Maui so soon?"

"We booked to leave at the end of the week, which we thought gave us plenty of time. We absolutely love our life there." Her mom beamed. "I have my tennis group and your father plays golf every second day. Then we both have bridge and canasta nights, and so many activities to keep us busy. I wish you could take some time off and come visit this summer. Bring Ty. Or George."

"I don't think you'd like George," Mila said with a subdued smile.

"Why not?" Her father narrowed his eyes. "He's not like that jumper you used to date, is he?"

"No," she sputtered, spewing wine. "George isn't married, if that's what you mean." So—her parents had known about her not-so-secret-affair. She'd thought she'd hidden her pain and the sordid details of her affair, but obviously not. Her parents had waited six years to allude to her misguided past, but they'd known.

"Okay. We just want you to be happy. Bring anyone you want."

"If George is one of your gay friends, we'd welcome him too," her mother said, patting her arm. "We're quite liberal, you know."

Mila felt like her parents had become other people. In a weird but good way. Still, all things considered, her vibrator seemed a safer subject than her married-jumper-ex-boyfriend. "George is not gay, nor is he a man, for that matter. And he'd be easy to bring. Would fit right in my bag."

Her mother pondered that for a moment, then her eyes grew big as saucers. "You mean….she's talking about one of those things," she told her husband. Her hand flew to her mouth, "Oh, my." She looked at her daughter, and her face broke into a grin. "My, my." She started to laugh, and Mila joined in.

CHAPTER TWENTY-FIVE

The wedding was outdoors in a garden area on the far side of the pool. It was a beautiful night and a perfect setting, with the snow-capped mountains in the background, the long fairway golf course view, and the magnificent hotel which resembled an old world European chateau.

The Grande Cascade had many weddings scheduled throughout the year at this particular location and an area with a picturesque Gazebo, designed for stunning photos. The justice of the peace presiding over the wedding stood with Devon inside the decorative Gazebo and Mila took her place next to Cindy. Kyle and Devon's best man, Josh, stood across from them, both looking dashing in their dark suits, slicked back hair, and clean shaven faces. Josh was a fellow ski patroller and paramedic in the area, and had been a skirt chaser for years.

He winked at Mila, who grinned and winked back. They had dated a few times, but never seriously. He was one of few men she'd call when she'd felt lonely.

Tara was escorted down the small flowered path toward the altar by her father, and looked so beautiful and happy that Mila got choked up inside. What was it about weddings that could reduce the coldest heart to tears? Even a non-romantic like herself got carried away in the moment; no wonder there were so many hook-ups between the single women and the groom's best friends.

Not tonight. Not for her. She had enough on her hands. Like how to let Ty down gently and remain as friends. She also had to figure out what to do with Chase, if he showed up at all.

Devon stood before the altar, facing the guests as he watched his bride stride toward him, her small hand tucked inside her father's arm. Tara's dad bent his head and whispered something to her, and she looked up at Devon and tossed him a kiss. The delighted guests cheered.

When she reached the gazebo, Devon took her hand and kissed the palm, and her father stepped aside. They'd each written their vows, which they now repeated in front of the small gathering, their eyes locked on each other. As they said their "I do's" Mila had to wipe away a mist of tears, and glanced around, seeing others scrambling for their tissues.

Once pronounced "bride and groom" the newlyweds turned to each other and kissed. And kissed.

Mila glanced around at the familiar faces, smiling with happiness, her heart filled with joy for her brother and his lovely new wife. The two of them held hands and walked back down the flowered path, waving and smiling at their friends and family in attendance. The bridesmaids and best men followed behind, while the guests threw rice and rose petals at the happy couple.

With the brief ceremony behind them, everyone gathered around the set up bar and mingled. Flutes of champagne were passed, and Ty quickly claimed his spot by Mila's side. He looked dashing tonight, wearing an expensive looking dark grey suit that complimented his thick black hair and slightly graying temples. He was an elegant man and very charming. She certainly could do a lot worse. And had.

He whispered something, and she leaned in close to hear his words. "You're looking luscious tonight," he said, slipping an arm around her waist and dropping a light kiss on her shoulder.

Startled, she jerked her head back, and it was then that she saw him, standing at the edge of the pool, watching the wedding from afar.

Chase was here. He'd come for her. She'd known he would.

"Ty." She teased him with a smile, wishing, hoping, Chase saw her acting happy. "Behave yourself. This is my brother's wedding, and I can't be the one having all the fun."

He laughed. "Play nice for as long as you want, but I have a big suite waiting."

She purposely took a long sip of champagne, wondering how to respond. "I have a nice room too, down the hall from my parents." She glanced around again, avoiding Chase entirely. Feeling him, though they were yards apart. "They are here only for a few days."

"Good people. I think they like me."

"Of course they do." Damn. So she couldn't use them for an excuse. Now what?

"You're a big girl. I'm sure they don't expect you not to date."

"I think you have something entirely different in mind." She dropped her eyes. "With them here, their room so close, I'd rather wait. Wouldn't you?"

"I'm sure they'd never know, or care if they did."

"I can't make promises. After all, I've only known you a short while."

She glanced behind him, wondering if Chase was still there. Would he come in, crash the party? What did he want anyway? Despite their love for one another, he knew they didn't have a future. They'd already discussed that over and over. Before he left.

On the other hand, Ty lived here. He worked at Mammoth and in Serendipity Falls. His construction business was doing great and now with all the new building going on, he'd be busier than ever.

If she wanted a future with someone, he was the right choice.

Even thinking this, she instinctively looked for Chase. Where was he? Had he left already, now that he knew she was okay and with another man? Would he give up that easily? Oh, where had chivalry gone? She wanted men to duel for her, not just turn around and walk away. Damn it! Such a ridiculous notion for a non-romantic girl. Must be the wedding getting to her.

She stiffened her spine, and tugged at her low cut gown, suddenly wishing it wasn't so revealing. She'd chosen the dress with Chase in mind. The sky was lit with stars, and a cool breeze blew. Mila shivered, and Ty picked up her wrap from a chair, draping it around her shoulders.

"Good thing we're eating inside," he said in a warm voice. "It's going to get cold tonight."

"It is, but it's lovely out here just the same." She handed him her empty glass. "Do you mind?"

"Not at all." Ty took her champagne glass and got in line in front of the bar. Waiters floated around with trays of canapés and finger food and Mila snagged a giant sized shrimp. She was ready to pop it in her mouth, when a voice behind her stopped her mid-air.

"Were you looking for me?"

She turned slowly. Chase. Her heart thundered. "What are you doing here?"

"You're not surprised to see me. Don't pretend. I know you better than that."

"We're done, Chase. You came to see if I was miserable or happy, not sure which." She shrugged, ignoring the shivers of expectation that skimmed along her skin. He was close enough to touch her. Would he dare? "But you can leave now. I'm happy. Okay?"

She plopped the shrimp in her mouth and chewed furiously. Swallowed. Wished she had her wine.

"No you're not, and neither am I." He took a step closer, bringing instant heat with him. "We're miserable without each other. I had to go home to figure that out— see if I could forget you or if you were really under my skin. You're under my skin, all right, and no amount of scrubbing is going to get you out."

She swallowed again, and tried to squash her inner excitement. "Oh, that's so romantic. You really know how to make a girl swoon."

"You're not the swooning type, and even if you were, I'd rather do this." He pulled her up against him and his mouth captured hers.

She couldn't move if she tried. Her knees all but gave way. She clung to his shoulder and accepted his kiss. Her eyes were closed and she didn't see what happened next, but suddenly Chase was pulled away from her.

"What do you think you're doing?" Ty had Chase by the collar, and she wasn't sure if the question had been directed at her or the man he was glowering at.

Chase shrugged him off. "I'm trying to convince her that I'm here to stay."

"She doesn't want you." Ty's face had darkened and he shot her a questioning look. "Tell him Mila."

She put her hands to her face. Her cheeks were flaming hot, but inside she felt so cold. She hated to be cruel and hurt people. She should have come alone and not led him on.

Too late now. "I would, but I can't. I'm so sorry." She searched Ty's face, hoping for a little understanding. "It's complicated. To do with the love bug."

Chase smiled and Ty swung at him, missing his chin by an inch. "Get lost," he snarled. "This is a private party."

Tara hurried over, looking like a roman goddess in her wedding gown. "Is there a problem?"

Ty straightened his tie, and put back his broad shoulders. "Not from me, but this jerk crashed your wedding and won't leave."

Chase slid up next to Mila, and put a protective hand on her back. "Tara, congratulations on your wedding. Sorry, if we caused a disturbance. I'll leave right now if Mila wants me to."

Tara looked at both men, then smiled at Mila, as if to say she told her so. "Which one will it be?"

Mila bit her lip and looked down at her feet, instinctively moving closer to Chase. "Ty, I'm sorry but I still have some unfinished business with Chase. He's the reporter I told you about." She'd been honest about her feelings for Chase from the beginning, but Ty had ignored her warnings.

"Yeah, I got that. You're making one hell of a mistake." He threw Chase a threatening look and then pushed his way past the wedding party. On his way out, he turned to face the guests. "What are you all looking at?"

"Well, that's an ugly side of him I never saw," Tara said sweetly. "Chase, please help yourself to a drink, and stay for dinner. The seat next to Mila is empty."

"Don't mind if I do," he answered, and pulled Mila a step closer. "What shall we drink to," he asked in a low voice.

The inevitable? Or free choice? Or love, guided by an angel's hand?

"That depends," Mila said, feeling happier than she'd ever felt in her life –including her time with Lucky Lady. "What are you asking?"

"I'm asking how we can make this thing work, because the one thing I know is that I don't want to live without you. Not another day if I can help it."

She gave a slow blink, knowing she'd go wherever he wanted, while hoping against hope that he'd stay in Serendipity. "Do you still want to go overseas?"

"Not anymore. I want to be where you are." He ran his finger across her shoulder. "I want to spend my life with you."

She smiled. "Is that some kind of proposal?"

"If you'll accept, it sure is."

"Chicken." She grinned. "Kiss me and then I'll decide."

He didn't have to be asked twice. He kissed her long and hard, and she could hear claps and shouts of encouragement from the wedding guests. She pulled back long enough to smile up at him. "I think we have everyone's approval."

Chase swung her around, keeping her close. "What about yours? Can you let go of the past, and take a chance on us?"

"Yes. I'd even move to Timbuktu, if that was the only way I could have you." She put her hands behind his head, and ran her fingers through his hair. "I love you, Chase Carlton from WUX News. And we will figure this out, one way or another."

"I love you, Mila O'Reilley, and forget Timbuktu, all I need is to be close to you." He kissed her cheek and murmured, "Serendipity is my home now. I feel responsible about what happens, and I aim to make sure that the gold is protected and the crater site is preserved."

"How are you going to do that?"

"Heck if I know. Maybe I'll elect myself mayor of this new boom town."

She laughed. "That's one of the things I love about you. You have incredible dreams."

"Meeting you has changed everything I thought I wanted, or needed. But before I go any further, I have a confession to make. My dad wasn't really a correspondent. And my brother died drunk driving into a pole."

"Chase! But you said -"

"I know. I stretched the truth a bit. You see, my whole adult life I've been trying to outrun my past and make a name for myself, but I'm done with that now. I don't want notoriety or money or fame. I don't want anything but you." He cupped her face and looked into her eyes. "You see, I couldn't work, I couldn't surf without wishing I was in the mountains, with a certain dark haired business woman and a rat eating cat."

She rested her head against his chest, his thumping heart. "Me too. That's all I want. Just you."

"I have something special waiting for you upstairs. But you can't wear it now. Not at this wedding." He kissed the top of her head, then stepped gently away.

Mila grabbed his hand. "You don't need to give me anything. You're enough, just as you are. Come, let's mingle with the guests and stop stealing the show."

"I have a better idea. Why don't you introduce me to Mom and Dad? They should meet their new son-in-law, shouldn't they?"

"Hmm, yes. Imagine. Today they've gained a daughter and now they'll add another prospective son."

"Forget the prospective part. I want to marry you as soon as we can. Is next weekend too soon?"

Her eyes widened, and then she laughed. "You really do have the wedding fever, don't you?"

"Let's get married before your folks go back to Hawaii." He swung her around in his arms. "How does that sound?"

"We can't get married that soon."

"Why not? You're the wedding planner, aren't you?" He winked. "And the ring is waiting upstairs. I know green is your favorite color."

"The moldavite. I saw the pictures in your article. It's a beautiful stone. I don't think anything could be more perfect. How did you know?"

"I knew." Chase lifted his head toward the sky.

She heard him whisper to some unknown source, "Thanks, pal. Your secret is safe with me."

"Who were you talking to?" She tilted her head and looked upward. Was he talking to that angel of hers?

"Just thanking the universe and anyone else up there for bringing me here to Serendipity and to you."

"Ditto that." She gazed into his eyes. "I love you so much, and now I know what this frenzy's all about. Being in love is the greatest feeling in the world."

"Now you have to plan our wedding for next week." He put an arm around her waist and whispered, "Don't want you too tired for our wedding night. Maybe we should elope?"

"That's a fantastic idea. I know just the place."

He looked confused. "Where in the world is better than here?"

"A honeymoon place. With sand and surf and a great big ocean." She grinned. "Let's go to Maui. Dev and Tara will already be there."

"We'll have to talk to your parents about that." He grabbed her hand. "Your father is throwing daggers my way. Let's do it now before he shoots me."

"Not to worry," she laughed. "If he accepted George, you're a shoo-in."

"Who the heck is George?"

"You met him. My bestseller back at the shop."

"You're kidding me, right?" When she shook her head no, he gave her a threatening look. "You can officially retire this George. Tell him you've got a real man for the job."

She laughed. "I fired him two weeks ago. He's with waste management now."

His dimples flashed. "Glad to hear it."

"Well, you know what they say. Once you've been Chased, there's no turning back."

CUPID

I just love happy endings, don't you?

Chase and Mila will figure this out and find a mutually satisfying solution to their geographical needs. After all, it isn't a plot of land that will bring them ever lasting happiness but their true, deep abiding love for each other. Chase has grown into a strong, courageous young man and Mila has finally forgiven herself for past transgressions and has opened her heart to love.

Love conquers all. It is the only true need that all humans have. Not wealth, not power, not possessions of any kind.

Love is all we need.

COMING SOON—The third book in this romantic comedy series—A COUGAR FOR KYLE. Watch for it next September or join my mailing list for a news release.

A NOTE FROM THE AUTHOR

Thank you for reading WEDDING FEVER, the second book in my Serendipity Falls romantic comedy series.

If you enjoyed this book, I'd appreciate it if you'd help others find it so they can enjoy it too.

• Lend it: This e-book is lending-enabled, so feel free to share it with your friends.

• Recommend it: Please help other readers find this book by recommending it to friends, readers' groups, and discussion boards.

• Review it: Let other potential readers know what you liked or didn't like about.

If you'd like to sign up for Patrice Wilton's newsletter to receive new release information, please visit www.patricewilton.com

You can follow Patrice Wilton on Facebook or on Twitter. @patricewilton

Book updates can be found at www.patricewilton.com.
I would love to hear from you at patricewilt@yahoo.com.

www.ingramcontent.com/pod-product-compliance
Lightning Source LLC
Chambersburg PA
CBHW070625130626
46556CB00001B/471